⟨⟩ **W9-BLS-244**

Praise for
Clive Barker's BOOKS OF BLOOD

"Our most accomplished contemporary purveyor of horror fiction." —*The New York Times Book Review*

"He scares even me. . . . What Barker does in the *Books of Blood* makes the rest of us look like we've been asleep for the last ten years. Some of the stories were so creepily awful that I literally could not read them alone; others go up and over the edge and into gruesome territory. . . . He's an original." —Stephen King

"Barker's dark, powerful imagination—and his skill in pacing to keep the stories surprising—make the horror grisly and effective." —*People*

"Barker's eye is unblinking; he drags out our terrors from the shadows and forces us to look upon them and despair or laugh with relief." —*The Washington Post*

"Ever since the heyday of horror fiction, when Henry James and Edith Wharton tried their hands at the supernatural, aficionados have been awaiting a writer to transcend the genre and give it new legitimacy. Clive Barker may be that man . . . witty, unpredictable, and concise. . . . Each story involves an uncanny mix of eroticism and terror." —*Time*

"Mixing elements of horror, science fiction, and surrealist literature, Barker's work reads like a cross between Stephen King and South American novelist Gabriel García Márquez. He creates a world where our biggest fears appear to be our own dreams."   —*Boston Herald*

"Clive Barker assaults our senses and our psyche, seeking not so much to tingle our spine as to snap it altogether."
—*Los Angeles Times*

"Clive Barker redefines the horror tale in his *Books of Blood*, bringing new beauty to ghastliness and new subtleties to terror."   —*Locus*

BOOKS BY CLIVE BARKER

Novels
THE DAMNATION GAME
WEAVEWORLD
THE GREAT AND SECRET SHOW
THE HELLBOUND HEART
IMAJICA
EVERVILLE
SACRAMENT
GALILEE
COLDHEART CANYON
MISTER B. GONE
THE SCARLET GOSPELS

Short Stories
BOOKS OF BLOOD, VOLUMES ONE TO THREE
IN THE FLESH
THE INHUMAN CONDITION
CABAL

For Children
THE THIEF OF ALWAYS
ABARAT
ABARAT: DAYS OF MAGIC, NIGHTS OF WAR
ABARAT: ABSOLUTE MIDNIGHT

Artwork
IMAGINER, VOLUMES ONE TO EIGHT

AUTHOR WEBSITE: WWW.CLIVEBARKER.INFO

CLIVE BARKER'S

BOOKS
OF
BLOOD

-Volume One-

BERKLEY
New York

BERKLEY
An imprint of Penguin Random House LLC
penguinrandomhouse.com

Copyright © 1984 by Clive Barker
Published by arrangement with Sphere Books.
Penguin Random House supports copyright. Copyright fuels creativity, encourages
diverse voices, promotes free speech, and creates a vibrant culture. Thank you for buying
an authorized edition of this book and for complying with copyright laws by not
reproducing, scanning, or distributing any part of it in any form without permission.
You are supporting writers and allowing Penguin Random House to continue to
publish books for every reader.

BERKLEY and the BERKLEY & B colophon are registered trademarks
of Penguin Random House LLC.

ISBN: 9780593201053

Berkley mass-market edition / June 1986
Berkley mass-market movie tie-in edition / September 2020

Printed in the United States of America
1 3 5 7 9 10 8 6 4 2

Book design by George Towne

This is a work of fiction. Names, characters, places, and incidents either are the product
of the author's imagination or are used fictitiously, and any resemblance to actual persons,
living or dead, business establishments, events, or locales is entirely coincidental.

If you purchased this book without a cover, you should be aware that this book is stolen
property. It was reported as "unsold and destroyed" to the publisher, and neither the author
nor the publisher has received any payment for this "stripped book."

EVERYBODY IS A BOOK OF BLOOD;
WHEREVER WE'RE OPENED, WE'RE RED.

Clive Barker's
BOOKS OF BLOOD
-Volume One-

THE BOOK OF BLOOD

T HE DEAD HAVE HIGHWAYS.

They run, unerring lines of ghost-trains, of dream-carriages, across the wasteland behind our lives, bearing an endless traffic of departed souls. Their thrum and throb can be heard in the broken places of the world, through cracks made by acts of cruelty, violence and depravity. Their freight, the wandering dead, can be glimpsed when the heart is close to bursting, and sights that should be hidden come plainly into view.

They have signposts, these highways, and bridges and lay-bys. They have turnpikes and intersections.

It is at these intersections, where the crowds of dead

mingle and cross, that this forbidden highway is most likely to spill through into our world. The traffic is heavy at the crossroads, and the voices of the dead are at their most shrill. Here the barriers that separate one reality from the next are worn thin with the passage of innumerable feet.

Such an intersection on the highway of the dead was located at Number 65, Tollington Place. Just a brick-fronted, mock-Georgian detached house, Number 65 was unremarkable in every other way. An old, forgettable house, stripped of the cheap grandeur it had once laid claim to, it had stood empty for a decade or more.

It was not rising damp that drove tenants from Number 65. It was not the rot in the cellars, or the subsidence that had opened a crack in the front of the house that ran from doorstep to eaves, it was the noise of passage. In the upper story the din of that traffic never ceased. It cracked the plaster on the walls and it warped the beams. It rattled the windows. It rattled the mind too. Number 65, Tollington Place, was a haunted house, and no one could possess it for long without insanity setting in.

At some time in its history a horror had been committed in that house. No one knew when, or what. But even to the untrained observer the oppressive atmosphere of the house, particularly the top story, was unmistakable. There was a memory and a promise of blood in the air of Number 65, a scent that lingered in the sinuses, and turned the strongest stomach. The building and its environs were shunned by vermin, by birds, even by flies. No wood lice crawled in its kitchen, no starling had nested in its attic. Whatever violence had been done there, it had opened the house up, as surely as a knife slits a fish's belly; and through that cut, that wound in the world, the dead peered out, and had their say.

That was the rumor anyway . . .

꧁

IT WAS THE THIRD WEEK OF THE INVESTIGATION at 65 Tollington Place. Three weeks of unprecedented success in the realm of the paranormal. Using a newcomer to the business, a twenty-year-old called Simon McNeal, as a medium, the Essex University Parapsychology Unit had recorded all but incontrovertible evidence of life after death.

In the top room of the house, a claustrophobic corridor of a room, the McNeal boy had apparently summoned the dead, and at his request they had left copious evidence of their visits, writing in a hundred different hands on the pale ochre walls. They wrote, it seemed, whatever came into their heads. Their names, of course, and their birth and death dates. Fragments of memories, and well-wishes to their living descendants, strange elliptical phrases that hinted at their present torments and mourned their lost joys. Some of the hands were square and ugly, some delicate and feminine. There were obscene drawings and half-finished jokes alongside lines of romantic poetry. A badly drawn rose. A game of noughts and crosses. A shopping list.

The famous had come to this wailing wall—Mussolini was there, Lennon and Janis Joplin—and nobodies too, forgotten people, had signed themselves beside the greats. It was a roll call of the dead, and it was growing day by day, as though word of mouth was spreading amongst the lost tribes, and seducing them out of silence to sign this barren room with their sacred presence.

❧

AFTER A LIFETIME'S WORK IN THE FIELD OF psychic research, Doctor Florescu was well accustomed to the hard facts of failure. It had been almost comfortable, settling back into a certainty that the evidence would never manifest itself. Now, faced with a sudden and spectacular success, she felt both elated and confused.

She sat, as she had sat for three incredible weeks, in the main room on the middle floor, one flight of stairs down from the writing room, and listened to the clamor of noises from upstairs with a sort of awe, scarcely daring to believe that she was allowed to be present at this miracle. There had been nibbles before, tantalizing hints of voices from another world, but this was the first time that province had insisted on being heard.

Upstairs, the noises stopped.

Mary looked at her watch: it was six-seventeen p.m.

For some reason best known to the visitors, the contact never lasted much after six. She'd wait 'til half-past, then go up. What would it have been today? Who would have come to that sordid little room and left their mark?

"Shall I set up the cameras?" Reg Fuller, her assistant, asked.

"Please," she murmured, distracted by expectation.

"Wonder what we'll get today?"

"We'll leave him ten minutes."

"Sure."

Upstairs, McNeal slumped in the corner of the room, and watched the October sun through the tiny window. He felt a little shut in, all alone in that damn place, but he still smiled to himself, that wan, beatific smile that melted even the most academic heart. Especially Doctor Florescu's: oh yes, the woman was infatuated with his smile, his eyes, the lost look he put on for her . . .

It was a fine game.

Indeed, at first that was all it had been—a game. Now Simon knew they were playing for bigger stakes; what had begun as a sort of lie-detection test had turned into a very serious contest: McNeal versus the Truth. The truth was simple: he was a cheat. He penned all his "ghost-writings" on the wall with tiny shards of lead he secreted under his tongue: he banged and thrashed and shouted without any provocation other than the sheer mischief of it: and the unknown names he wrote, ha, he laughed to think of it, the names he found in telephone directories.

Yes, it was indeed a fine game.

She promised him so much, she tempted him with fame, encouraging every lie that he invented. Promises of wealth, of applauded appearances on the television, of an adulation he'd never known before. As long as he produced the ghosts.

He smiled the smile again. She called him her Go-Between: an innocent carrier of messages. She'd be up the stairs soon—her eyes on his body, her voice close to tears with her pathetic excitement at another series of scrawled names and nonsense.

He liked it when she looked at his nakedness, or all but nakedness. All his sessions were carried out with him only dressed in a pair of briefs, to preclude any hidden aids. A ridiculous precaution. All he needed were the leads under his tongue, and enough energy to fling himself around for half an hour, bellowing his head off.

He was sweating. The groove of his breastbone was slick with it, his hair plastered to his pale forehead. Today had been hard work: he was looking forward to getting out of the room, sluicing himself down and basking in admiration awhile. The Go-Between put his hand down his briefs and played with himself, idly. Somewhere in the room a fly, or flies maybe, was trapped. It was late in the season for flies, but he could hear them somewhere close. They buzzed and fretted against the window, or around the light bulb. He heard their tiny fly voices, but didn't question them, too engrossed in his thoughts of the game, and in the simple delight of stroking himself.

How they buzzed, these harmless insect voices, buzzed and sang and complained. How they complained.

Mary Florescu drummed the table with her fingers. Her wedding ring was loose today, she felt it moving with the rhythm of her tapping. Sometimes it was tight and sometimes loose: one of those small mysteries that she'd never analyzed properly but simply accepted. In fact today it was very loose: almost ready to fall off. She thought of Alan's face. Alan's dear face. She thought of it through a hole made of her wedding ring, as if down a tunnel. Was that what his death had been like: being carried away and yet further away down a tunnel to the dark? She thrust the ring deeper onto her hand. Through the tips of her index-finger and thumb she seemed almost to taste the sour metal as she touched it. It was a curious sensation, an illusion of some kind.

To wash the bitterness away she thought of the boy. His face came easily, so very easily, splashing into her consciousness with his smile and his unremarkable physique, still unmanly. Like a girl really—the roundness of him, the sweet clarity of his skin—the innocence.

9

Her fingers were still on the ring, and the sourness she had tasted grew. She looked up. Fuller was organizing the equipment. Around his balding head a nimbus of pale green light shimmered and wove—

She suddenly felt giddy.

Fuller saw nothing and heard nothing. His head was bowed to his business, engrossed. Mary stared at him still, seeing the halo on him, feeling new sensations waking in her, coursing through her. The air seemed suddenly alive: the very molecules of oxygen, hydrogen, nitrogen jostled against her in an intimate embrace. The nimbus around Fuller's head was spreading, finding fellow radiance in every object in the room. The unnatural sense in her fingertips was spreading too. She could see the color of her breath as she exhaled it: a pinky orange glamour in the bubbling air. She could hear, quite clearly, the voice of the desk she sat at: the low whine of its solid presence.

The world was opening up: throwing her senses into an ecstasy, coaxing them into a wild confusion of functions. She was capable, suddenly, of knowing the world as a system, not of politics or religions, but as a system of senses, a system that spread out from the living flesh to the inert wood of her desk, to the stale gold of her wedding ring.

And further. Beyond wood, beyond gold. The crack opened that led to the highway. In her head she heard voices that came from no living mouth.

She looked up, or rather some force thrust her head back violently and she found herself staring up at the ceiling. It was covered with worms. No. That was absurd! It *seemed* to be alive, though, maggoty with life—pulsing, dancing.

She could see the boy through the ceiling. He was sitting on the floor, with his jutting member in his hand. His head was thrown back, like hers. He was as lost in his ecstasy as she was. Her new sight saw the throbbing light in and around his body—traced the passion that was seated in his gut, and his head molten with pleasure.

It saw another sight, the lie in him, the absence of power where she'd thought there had been something wonderful. He had no talent to commune with ghosts, nor had he ever had, she saw this plainly. He was a little liar, a boy-liar, a sweet, white boy-liar without the compassion or the wisdom to understand what he had dared to do.

Now it was done. The lies were told, the tricks were played, and the people on the highway, sick beyond death of being misrepresented and mocked, were buzzing at the crack in the wall, and demanding satisfaction.

That crack *she* had opened: *she* had unknowingly fingered and fumbled at, unlocking it by slow degrees. Her desire for the boy had done that: her endless thoughts of him, her frustration, her heat and her disgust at her heat had pulled the crack wider. Of all the powers that made the system manifest, love, and its companion, passion, and their companion, loss, were the most potent. Here she was, an embodiment of all three. Loving, and wanting, and sensing acutely the impossibility of the former two. Wrapped up in an agony of feeling which she had denied herself, believing she loved the boy simply as her Go-Between.

It wasn't true! It wasn't true! She wanted him, wanted him *now*, deep inside her. Except that now it was too late. The traffic could be denied no longer: it demanded, yes, it *demanded* access to the little trickster.

She was helpless to prevent it. All she could do was utter a tiny gasp of horror as she saw the highway open out before her, and understood that this was no common intersection they stood at.

Fuller heard the sound.

"Doctor?" He looked up from his tinkering and his face—washed with a blue light she could see from the corner of her eye—bore an expression of inquiry.

"Did you say something?" he asked.

She thought, with a fillip of her stomach, of how this was bound to end.

The ether-faces of the dead were quite clear in front of her. She could see the profundity of their suffering and she could sympathize with their ache to be heard.

She saw plainly that the highways that crossed at Tollington Place were not common thoroughfares. She was not staring at the happy, idling traffic of the ordinary dead. No, that house opened onto a route walked only by the victims and the perpetrators of violence. The men, the women, the children who had died enduring all the pains nerves had wit to muster, with their minds branded by the circumstances of their deaths. Eloquent beyond words, their eyes spoke their agonies, their ghost bodies still bearing the wounds that had killed them. She could also see, mingling freely with the innocents, their slaughterers and tormentors. These monsters, frenzied, mush-minded blood-letters, peeked through into the world: nonesuch creatures, unspoken, forbidden miracles of our species, chattering and howling their Jabberwocky.

Now the boy above her sensed them. She saw him turn a little in the silent room, knowing that the voices he heard were not fly-voices, the complaints were not insect-complaints. He was aware, suddenly, that he had lived in a tiny corner of the world, and that the rest of it, the Third, Fourth and Fifth Worlds, was pressing at his lying back, hungry and irrevocable. The sight of his panic was also a smell and a taste to her. Yes, she tasted him as she had always longed to, but it was not a kiss that married their senses, it was his growing panic. It filled her up: her empathy was total. The fearful glance was hers as much as his—their dry throats rasped the same small word:

"Please—"

That the child learns.

"Please—"

That wins care and gifts.

13

"Please—"

That even the dead, surely, even the dead must know and obey.

"Please—"

Today there would be no such mercy given, she knew for certain. The ghosts had despaired on the highway a grieving age, bearing the wounds they had died with, and the insanities they had slaughtered with. They had endured his levity and insolence, his idiocies, the fabrications that had made a game of their ordeals. They wanted to speak the truth.

Fuller was peering at her more closely, his face now swimming in a sea of pulsing orange light. She felt his hands on her skin. They tasted of vinegar.

"Are you all right?" he said, his breath like iron.

She shook her head.

No, she was not all right, nothing was right.

The crack was gaping wider every second: through it she could see another sky, the slate heavens that loured over the highway. It overwhelmed the mere reality of the house.

"Please," she said, her eyes rolling up to the fading substance of the ceiling.

Wider. Wider—

The brittle world she inhabited was stretched to breaking point.

Suddenly, it broke, like a dam, and the black waters poured through, inundating the room.

Fuller knew something was amiss (it was in the color of his aura, the sudden fear), but he didn't understand what was happening. She felt his spine ripple: she could see his brain whirl.

"What's going on?" he said. The pathos of the inquiry made her want to laugh.

Upstairs, the water-jug in the writing room shattered.

Fuller let her go and ran towards the door. It began to rattle and shake even as he approached it, as though all the inhabitants of hell were beating on the other side. The handle turned and turned and turned. The paint blistered. The key glowed red-hot.

Fuller looked back at the Doctor, who was still fixed in that grotesque position, head back, eyes wide.

He reached for the handle, but the door opened before he could touch it. The hallway beyond had disappeared altogether. Where the familiar interior had stood the vista of the highway stretched to the horizon. The sight killed Fuller in a moment. His mind had no strength to take the panorama in—it could not control the overload that ran through his every nerve. His heart stopped; a revolution overturned the order of his system; his bladder failed, his bowels failed, his limbs shook and collapsed. As he sank to the floor his face began to blister like the door, and his corpse rattle like the handle. He was inert stuff already: as fit for this indignity as wood or steel.

Somewhere to the east his soul joined the wounded

highway, on its route to the intersection where a moment previously he had died.

Mary Florescu knew she was alone. Above her the marvelous boy, her beautiful, cheating child, was writhing and screeching as the dead set their vengeful hands on his fresh skin. She knew their intention: she could see it in their eyes—there was nothing new about it. Every history had this particular torment in its tradition. He was to be used to record their testaments. He was to be their page, their book, the vessel for their autobiographies. A book of blood. A book made of blood. A book written in blood. She thought of the grimoires that had been made of dead human skin: she'd seen them, touched them. She thought of the tattoos she'd seen: freak show exhibits some of them, others just shirtless laborers in the street with a message to their mothers pricked across their backs. It was not unknown, to write a book of blood.

But on such skin, on such gleaming skin—oh God, that was the crime. He screamed as the torturing needles of broken jug-glass skipped against his flesh, ploughing it up. She felt his agonies as if they were hers, and they were not so terrible . . .

Yet he screamed. And fought, and poured obscenities out at his attackers. They took no notice. They swarmed around him, deaf to any plea or prayer, and worked on him with all the enthusiasm of creatures forced into silence for too long. Mary listened as his voice wearied with its complaints, and she fought against the weight of fear in her limbs. Somehow, she felt, she must get up to the room. It didn't matter what was beyond the door or on the stairs—he needed her, and that was enough.

She stood up and felt her hair swirl up from her head, flailing like the snake hair of the Gorgon Medusa. Reality swam—there was scarcely a floor to be seen beneath her. The boards of the house were ghost-wood, and beyond them a seething dark raged and yawned at her. She looked to the door, feeling all the time a lethargy that was so hard to fight off.

Clearly they didn't want her up there. Maybe, she thought, they even fear me a little. The idea gave her resolution; why else were they bothering to intimidate her unless her very presence, having once opened this hole in the world, was now a threat to them?

The blistered door was open. Beyond it the reality of the house had succumbed completely to the howling chaos of the highway. She stepped through, concentrating on the way her feet still touched solid floor even though her eyes could no longer see it. The sky above her was prussian blue, the highway was wide and windy, the dead pressed on every side. She fought through them as through a crowd of living people, while their gawping, idiot faces looked at her and hated her invasion.

The "please" was gone. Now she said nothing; just gritted her teeth and narrowed her eyes against the highway, kicking her feet forward to find the reality of the stairs that she knew were there. She tripped as she touched them, and a howl went up from the crowd. She couldn't tell if they were laughing at her clumsiness, or sounding a warning at how far she had got.

First step. Second step. Third step.

Though she was torn at from every side, she was winning against the crowd. Ahead she could see through the door of the room to where her little liar was sprawled, surrounded by his attackers. His briefs were around his ankles: the scene looked like a kind of rape. He screamed no longer, but his eyes were wild with terror and pain. At least he was still alive. The natural resilience of his young mind had half accepted the spectacle that had opened in front of him.

Suddenly his head jerked around and he looked straight through the door at her. In this extremity he had dredged up a true talent, a skill that was a fraction of Mary's, but enough to make contact with her. Their eyes met. In a sea of blue darkness, surrounded on every side with a civilization they neither knew nor understood, their living hearts met and married.

"I'm sorry," he said silently. It was infinitely pitiful. "I'm sorry. I'm sorry." He looked away, his gaze wrenched from hers.

She was certain she must be almost at the top of the stairs, her feet still treading air as far as her eyes could tell, the faces of the travelers above, below and on every side of her. But she could see, very faintly, the outline of

the door, and the boards and beams of the room where
Simon lay. He was one mass of blood now, from head to
foot. She could see the marks, the hieroglyphics of agony
on every inch of his torso, his face, his limbs. One
moment he seemed to flash into a kind of focus, and she
could see him in the empty room, with the sun through
the window, and the shattered jug at his side. Then her
concentration would falter and instead she'd see the
invisible world made visible, and he'd be hanging in the
air while they wrote on him from every side, plucking
out the hair on his head and body to clear the page,
writing in his armpits, writing on his eyelids, writing on
his genitals, in the crease of his buttocks, on the soles of
his feet.

Only the wounds were in common between the two
sights. Whether she saw him beset with authors, or alone
in the room, he was bleeding and bleeding.

She had reached the door now. Her trembling hand
stretched to touch the solid reality of the handle, but
even with all the concentration she could muster it would
not come clear. There was barely a ghost-image for her to
focus on, though it was sufficient. She grasped the
handle, turned it and flung the door of the writing room
open.

He was there, in front of her. No more than two or
three yards of possessed air separated them. Their eyes
met again, and an eloquent look, common to the living
and the dead worlds, passed between them. There was

compassion in that look, and love. The fictions fell away, the lies were dust. In place of the boy's manipulative smiles was a true sweetness—answered in her face.

And the dead, fearful of this look, turned their heads away. Their faces tightened, as though the skin was being stretched over the bone, their flesh darkening to a bruise, their voices becoming wistful with the anticipation of defeat. She reached to touch him, no longer having to fight against the hordes of the dead; they were falling away from their quarry on every side, like dying flies dropping from a window.

She touched him, lightly, on the face. The touch was a benediction. Tears filled his eyes, and ran down his scarified cheek, mingling with the blood.

The dead had no voices now, nor even mouths. They were lost along the highway, their malice damned.

Plane by plane the room began to reestablish itself. The floorboards became visible under his sobbing body, every nail, every stained plank. The windows came clearly into view—and outside the twilight street was echoing with the clamor of children. The highway had disappeared from living human sight entirely. Its travelers had turned their faces to the dark and gone away into oblivion, leaving only their signs and their talismans in the concrete world.

On the middle landing of Number 65 the smoking, blistered body of Reg Fuller was casually trodden by the travelers' feet as they passed over the intersection. At length Fuller's own soul came by in the throng and glanced down at the flesh he had once occupied, before the crowd pressed him on towards his judgement.

Upstairs, in the darkening room, Mary Florescu knelt beside the McNeal boy and stroked his blood-plastered head. She didn't want to leave the house for assistance until she was certain his tormentors would not come back. There was no sound now but the whine of a jet finding its way through the stratosphere to morning. Even the boy's breathing was hushed and regular. No nimbus of light surrounded him. Every sense was in place. Sight. Sound. Touch.

Touch.

She touched him now as she had never previously dared, brushing her fingertips, oh so lightly, over his body, running her fingers across the raised skin like a blind woman reading braille. There were minute words on every millimeter of his body, written in a multitude of hands. Even through the blood she could discern the meticulous way that the words had harrowed into him. She could even read, by the dimming light, an occasional phrase. It was proof beyond any doubt, and she wished, oh God how she wished, that she had not come by it. And yet, after a lifetime of waiting, here it was: the revelation of life beyond flesh, written in flesh itself.

The boy would survive, that was clear. Already the blood was drying, and the myriad wounds healing. He was healthy and strong, after all: there would be no

21

fundamental physical damage. His beauty was gone forever, of course. From now on he would be an object of curiosity at best, and at worst of repugnance and horror. But she would protect him, and he would learn, in time, how to know and trust her. Their hearts were inextricably tied together.

And after a time, when the words on his body were scabs and scars, she would read him. She would trace, with infinite love and patience, the stories the dead had told on him.

The tale on his abdomen, written in a fine, cursive style. The testimony in exquisite, elegant print that covered his face and scalp. The story on his back, and on his shins, on his hands.

She would read them all, report them all, every last syllable that glistened and seeped beneath her adoring fingers, so that the world would know the stories that the dead tell.

He was a Book of Blood, and she his sole translator.

As darkness fell, she left off her vigil and led him, naked, into the balmy night.

⹋

HERE THEN ARE THE STORIES WRITTEN ON THE Book of Blood. Read, if it pleases you, and learn.

They are a map of that dark highway that leads out of life towards unknown destinations. Few will have to take it. Most will go peacefully along lamplit streets, ushered out of living with prayers and caresses. But for a few, a chosen few, the horrors will come, skipping to fetch them off to the highway of the damned.

So read. Read and learn.

It's best to be prepared for the worst, after all, and wise to learn to walk before breath runs out.

THE MIDNIGHT

MEAT TRAIN

LEON KAUFMAN WAS NO LONGER NEW TO THE city. The Palace of Delights, he'd always called it, in the days of his innocence. But that was when he'd lived in Atlanta, and New York was still a kind of promised land, where anything and everything was possible.

Now Kaufman had lived three and a half months in his dream-city, and the Palace of Delights seemed less than delightful.

Was it really only a season since he stepped out of Port Authority Bus Station and looked up 42nd Street towards the Broadway intersection? So short a time to lose so many treasured illusions.

He was embarrassed now even to think of his naïveté. It made him wince to remember how he had stood and announced aloud: "New York, I love you."

Love? Never.

It had been at best an infatuation.

And now, after only three months living with his object of adoration, spending his days and nights in her presence, she had lost her aura of perfection.

New York was just a city.

He had seen her wake in the morning like a slut, and pick murdered men from between her teeth, and suicides from the tangles of her hair. He had seen her late at night, her dirty back streets shamelessly courting depravity. He had watched her in the hot afternoon, sluggish and ugly, indifferent to the atrocities that were being committed every hour in her throttled passages.

It was no Palace of Delights.

It bred death, not pleasure.

Everyone he met had brushed with violence; it was a fact of life. It was almost chic to have known someone who had died a violent death. It was proof of living in that city.

But Kaufman had loved New York from afar for almost twenty years. He'd planned his love affair for most of his adult life. It was not easy, therefore, to shake the passion off, as though he had never felt it. There were still times, very early, before the cop-sirens began, or at twilight, when Manhattan was still a miracle.

For those moments, and for the sake of his dreams, he still gave her the benefit of the doubt, even when her behavior was less than lady-like.

⊰⊱

SHE DIDN'T MAKE SUCH FORGIVENESS EASY. IN the few months that Kaufman had lived in New York her streets had been awash with spilt blood.

In fact, it was not so much the streets themselves, but the tunnels beneath those streets.

"Subway Slaughter" was the catchphrase of the month. Only the previous week another three killings had been reported. The bodies had been discovered in one of the subway cars on the Avenue of the Americas, hacked open and partially disemboweled, as though an efficient abattoir operative had been interrupted in his work. The killings were so thoroughly professional that the Police were interviewing every man in their records who had some past connection with the butchery trade. The meat-packaging plants on the waterfront were being watched, the slaughterhouses scoured for clues. A swift arrest was promised, though none was made.

This recent trio of corpses was not the first to be discovered in such a state; the very day that Kaufman had arrived a story had broken in the *Times* that was still the talk of every morbid secretary in the office.

The story went that a German visitor, lost in the subway

system late at night, had come across a body in a train. The victim was a well-built, attractive thirty-year-old woman from Brooklyn. She had been completely stripped. Every shred of clothing, every article of jewelery. Even the studs in her ears.

More bizarre than the stripping was the neat and systematic way in which the clothes had been folded and placed in individual plastic bags on the seat beside the corpse.

This was no irrational slasher at work. This was a highly organized mind: a lunatic with a strong sense of tidiness.

Further, and yet more bizarre than the careful stripping of the corpse, was the outrage that had then been perpetrated upon it. The reports claimed, though the Police Department failed to confirm this, that the body had been meticulously shaved. Every hair had been removed: from the head, from the groin, from beneath the arms; all cut and scorched back to the flesh. Even the eyebrows and eyelashes had been plucked out.

Finally, this all too naked slab had been hung by the feet from one of the holding handles set in the roof of the car, and a black plastic bucket, lined with a black plastic bag, had been placed beneath the corpse to catch the steady fall of blood from its wounds.

In that state, stripped, shaved, suspended and practically bled white, the body of Loretta Dyer had been found.

It was disgusting, it was meticulous and it was deeply confusing.

There had been no rape, nor any sign of torture. The woman had been swiftly and efficiently dispatched as though she was a piece of meat. And the butcher was still loose.

The City Fathers, in their wisdom, declared a complete closedown on press reports of the slaughter. It was said that the man who had found the body was in protective custody in New Jersey, out of sight of inquiring journalists. But the cover-up had failed. Some greedy cop had leaked the salient details to a reporter from the *Times*. Everyone in New York now knew the horrible story of the slaughters. It was a topic of conversation in every Deli and bar; and, of course, on the subway.

But Loretta Dyer was only the first.

Now three more bodies had been found in identical circumstances; though the work had clearly been interrupted on this occasion. Not all the bodies had been shaved, and the jugulars had not been severed to bleed them. There was another, more significant difference in the discovery: it was not a tourist who had stumbled on the sight, it was a reporter from the *New York Times*.

Kaufman surveyed the report that sprawled across the front page of the newspaper. He had no prurient interest in the story, unlike his elbow mate along the counter of the Deli. All he felt was a mild disgust that made him push his plate of over-cooked eggs aside. It was simply further proof of his city's decadence. He could take no pleasure in her sickness.

Nevertheless, being human, he could not entirely ignore the gory details on the page in front of him. The article was unsensationally written, but the simple clarity of the style made the subject seem more appalling. He couldn't help wondering, too, about the man behind the atrocities. Was there one psychotic loose, or several, each inspired to copy the original murder? Perhaps this was only the beginning of the horror. Maybe more murders would follow, until at last the murderer, in his exhilaration or exhaustion, would step beyond caution and be taken. Until then the city, Kaufman's adored city, would live in a state somewhere between hysteria and ecstasy.

At his elbow a bearded man knocked over Kaufman's coffee.

"Shit!" he said.

Kaufman shifted on his stool to avoid the dribble of coffee running off the counter.

"Shit," the man said again.

"No harm done," said Kaufman.

He looked at the man with a slightly disdainful expression on his face. The clumsy bastard was attempting to soak up the coffee with a napkin, which was turning to mush as he did so.

Kaufman found himself wondering if this oaf, with his florid cheeks and his uncultivated beard, was capable of murder. Was there any sign on that over-fed face, any clue in the shape of his head or the turn of his small eyes, that gave his true nature away?

The man spoke.

"Wannanother?"

Kaufman shook his head.

"Coffee. Regular. Dark," the oaf said to the girl behind the counter. She looked up from cleaning the grill of cold fat.

"Huh?"

"Coffee. You deaf?"

The man grinned at Kaufman.

"Deaf," he said.

Kaufman noticed he had three teeth missing from his lower jaw.

"Looks bad, huh?" he said.

What did he mean? The coffee? The absence of his teeth?

"Three people like that. Carved up."

Kaufman nodded.

"Makes you think," he said.

"Sure."

"I mean, it's a cover-up, isn't it? They know who did it."

This conversation's ridiculous, thought Kaufman. He took off his spectacles and pocketed them: the bearded face was no longer in focus. That was some improvement at least.

"Bastards," he said. "Fucking bastards, all of them. I'll lay you anything it's a cover-up."

33

"Of what?"

"They got the evidence: they're just keeping us in the fucking dark. There's something out there that's not human."

Kaufman understood. It was a conspiracy theory the oaf was trotting out. He'd heard them so often; a panacea.

"See, they do all this cloning stuff and it gets out of hand. They could be growing fucking monsters for all we know. There's something down there they won't tell us about. Cover-up, like I say. Lay you anything."

Kaufman found the man's certainty attractive. Monsters on the prowl. Six heads: a dozen eyes. Why not?

He knew why not. Because that excused his city: that let her off the hook. And Kaufman believed in his heart that the monsters to be found in the tunnels were perfectly human.

The bearded man threw his money on the counter and got up, sliding his fat bottom off the stained plastic stool.

"Probably a fucking cop," he said, as his parting shot. "Tried to make a fucking hero, made a fucking monster instead." He grinned grotesquely. "Lay you anything," he continued and lumbered out without another word.

Kaufman slowly exhaled through his nose, feeling the tension in his body abate.

He hated that sort of confrontation: it made him feel

tongue-tied and ineffectual. Come to think of it, he hated that kind of man: the opinionated brute that New York bred so well.

✦

IT WAS COMING UP TO SIX WHEN MAHOGANY woke. The morning rain had turned into a light drizzle by twilight. The air was about as clear-smelling as it ever got in Manhattan. He stretched on his bed, threw off the dirty blanket and got up for work.

In the bathroom the rain was dripping on the box of the air conditioner, filling the apartment with a rhythmical slapping sound. Mahogany turned on the television to cover the noise, disinterested in anything it had to offer.

He went to the window. The street six floors below was thick with traffic and people.

After a hard day's work New York was on its way home: to play, to make love. People were streaming out of their offices and into their automobiles. Some would be testy after a day's sweaty labor in a badly aired office; others, benign as sheep, would be wandering home down the Avenues, ushered along by a ceaseless current of bodies. Still others would even now be cramming onto the subway, blind to the graffiti on every wall, deaf to the babble of their own voices, and to the cold thunder of the tunnels.

It pleased Mahogany to think of that. He was, after all, not one of the common herd. He could stand at his window and look down on a thousand heads below him, and know he was a chosen man.

He had deadlines to meet, of course, like the people in the street. But his work was not their senseless labor, it was more like a sacred duty.

He needed to live, and sleep, and shit like them, too. But it was not financial necessity that drove him, but the demands of history.

He was in a great tradition, that stretched further back than America. He was a night-stalker: like Jack the Ripper, like Gilles de Rais, a living embodiment of death, a wraith with a human face. He was a haunter of sleep, and an awakener of terrors.

The people below him could not know his face; nor would care to look twice at him. But his stare caught them, and weighed them up, selecting only the ripest from the passing parade, choosing only the healthy and the young to fall under his sanctified knife.

Sometimes Mahogany longed to announce his identity to the world, but he had responsibilities and they bore on him heavily. He couldn't expect fame. His was a secret life, and it was merely pride that longed for recognition.

After all, he thought, does the beef salute the butcher as it throbs to its knees?

All in all, he was content. To be part of that great

tradition was enough, would always have to remain enough.

Recently, however, there had been discoveries. They weren't his fault of course. Nobody could possibly blame him. But it was a bad time. Life was not as easy as it had been ten years ago. He was that much older, of course, and that made the job more exhausting; and more and more the obligations weighed on his shoulders. He was a chosen man, and that was a difficult privilege to live with.

He wondered, now and then, if it wasn't time to think about training a younger man for his duties. There would need to be consultations with the Fathers, but sooner or later a replacement would have to be found, and it would be, he felt, a criminal waste of his experience not to take on an apprentice.

There were so many felicities he could pass on. The tricks of his extraordinary trade. The best way to stalk, to cut, to strip, to bleed. The best meat for the purpose. The simplest way to dispose of the remains. So much detail, so much accumulated expertise.

Mahogany wandered into the bathroom and turned on the shower. As he stepped in he looked down at his body. The small paunch, the greying hairs on his sagging chest, the scars and pimples that littered his pale skin. He was getting old. Still, tonight, like every other night, he had a job to do . . .

❖

KAUFMAN HURRIED BACK INTO THE LOBBY WITH his sandwich, turning down his collar and brushing rain off his hair. The clock above the elevator read seven-sixteen. He would work through until ten, no later.

The elevator took him up to the twelfth floor and to the Pappas offices. He traipsed unhappily through the maze of empty desks and hooded machines to his little territory, which was still illuminated. The women who cleaned the offices were chatting down the corridor: otherwise the place was lifeless.

He took off his coat, shook the rain off it as best he could and hung it up.

Then he sat down in front of the piles of orders he had been tussling with for the best part of three days, and began work. It would only take one more night's labor, he felt sure, to break the back of the job, and he found it easier to concentrate without the incessant clatter of typists and typewriters on every side.

He unwrapped his ham on whole wheat with extra mayonnaise and settled in for the evening.

❖

IT WAS NINE NOW.

Mahogany was dressed for the nightshift. He had his usual sober suit on, with his brown tie neatly knotted, his silver cufflinks (a gift from his first wife) placed in the sleeves of his immaculately pressed shirt, his thinning hair gleaming with oil, his nails snipped and polished, his face flushed with cologne.

His bag was packed. The towels, the instruments, his chain-mail apron.

He checked his appearance in the mirror. He could, he thought, still be taken for a man of forty-five, fifty at the outside.

As he surveyed his face he reminded himself of his duty. Above all, he must be careful. There would be eyes on him every step of the way, watching his performance tonight, and judging it. He must walk out like an innocent, arousing no suspicion.

If they only knew, he thought. The people who walked, ran and skipped past him on the streets: who collided with him without apology: who met his gaze with contempt: who smiled at his bulk, looking uneasy in his ill-fitting suit. If only they knew what he did, what he was and what he carried.

Caution, he said to himself, and turned off the light. The apartment was dark. He went to the door and opened it, used to walking in blackness. Happy in it.

The rain clouds had cleared entirely. Mahogany made his way down Amsterdam towards the subway at 145th Street. Tonight he'd take the Avenue of the Americas again, his favorite line and often the most productive.

Down the subway steps, token in hand. Through the

automatic gates. The smell of the tunnels was in his nostrils now. Not the smell of the deep tunnels of course. They had a scent all of their own. But there was reassurance even in the stale electric air of this shallow line. The regurgitated breath of a million travelers circulated in this warren, mingling with the breath of creatures far older; things with voices soft like clay, whose appetites were abominable. How he loved it. The scent, the dark, the thunder.

He stood on the platform and scanned his fellow travelers critically. There were one or two bodies he contemplated following, but there was so much dross amongst them: so few worth the chase. The physically wasted, the obese, the ill, the weary. Bodies destroyed by excess and by indifference. As a professional it sickened him, though he understood the weakness that spoiled the best of men.

He lingered in the station for over an hour, wandering between platforms while the trains came and went, came and went, and the people with them. There was so little of quality around it was dispiriting. It seemed he had to wait longer and longer every day to find flesh worthy of use.

It was now almost half past ten and he had not seen a single creature who was really ideal for slaughter.

No matter, he told himself, there was time yet. Very soon the theater crowd would be emerging. They were always good for a sturdy body or two. The well-fed intelligentsia, clutching their ticket-stubs and opining on the diversions of art—oh yes, there'd be something there.

If not, and there were nights when it seemed he would never find something suitable, he'd have to ride downtown and corner a couple of lovers out late, or find an athlete or two, fresh from one of the gyms. They were always sure to offer good material, except that with such healthy specimens there was always the risk of resistance.

He remembered catching two black bucks a year ago or more, with maybe forty years between them, father and son perhaps. They'd resisted with knives, and he'd been hospitalized for six weeks. It had been a close-fought encounter and one that had set him doubting his skills. Worse, it had made him wonder what his masters would have done with him had he suffered a fatal injury. Would he have been delivered to his family in New Jersey, and given a decent Christian burial? Or would his carcass have been thrown into the dark, for their own use?

The headline of the *New York Post*, discarded on the seat across from him, caught Mahogany's eye: "Police All-Out to Catch Killer." He couldn't resist a smile. Thoughts of failure, weakness and death evaporated. After all, he was that man, that killer, and tonight the thought of capture was laughable. After all, wasn't his career sanctioned by the highest possible authorities? No policeman could hold him, no court pass judgement on him. The very forces of law and order that made such a show of his pursuit served his masters no less than he; he almost wished some two-bit cop would catch him, take him in triumph before the judge, just to see the looks on their faces when the word came up from the dark that Mahogany was a protected man, above every law on the statute books.

It was now well after ten-thirty. The trickle of theatergoers had begun, but there was nothing likely so far. He'd want to let the rush pass anyway: just follow one or two choice pieces to the end of the line. He bided his time, like any wise hunter.

⁂

KAUFMAN WAS NOT FINISHED BY ELEVEN, AN hour after he'd promised himself release. But exasperation and ennui were making the job more difficult, and the sheets of figures were beginning to blur in front of him. At ten past eleven he threw down his pen and admitted defeat. He rubbed his hot eyes with the cushions of his palms 'til his head filled with colors.

"Fuck it," he said.

He never swore in company. But once in a while to say fuck it to himself was a great consolation. He made his way out of the office, damp coat over his arm, and headed for the elevator. His limbs felt drugged and his eyes would scarcely stay open.

It was colder outside than he had anticipated, and the

air brought him out of his lethargy a little. He walked towards the subway at 34th Street. Catch an Express to Far Rockaway. Home in an hour.

⁜

NEITHER KAUFMAN NOR MAHOGANY KNEW IT, but at 96th and Broadway the Police had arrested what they took to be the Subway Killer, having trapped him in one of the uptown trains. A small man of European extraction, wielding a hammer and a saw, had cornered a young woman in the second car and threatened to cut her in half in the name of Jehovah.

Whether he was capable of fulfilling this threat was doubtful. As it was, he didn't get the chance. While the rest of the passengers (including two Marines) looked on, the intended victim landed a kick to the man's testicles. He dropped the hammer. She picked it up and broke his lower jaw and right cheek-bone with it before the Marines stepped in.

When the train halted at 96th the Police were waiting to arrest the Subway Butcher. They rushed the car in a horde, yelling like banshees and scared as shit. The Butcher was lying in one corner of the car with his face in pieces. They carted him away, triumphant. The woman, after questioning, went home with the Marines.

It was to be a useful diversion, though Mahogany couldn't know it at the time. It took the Police the best part of the night to determine the identity of their prisoner, chiefly because he couldn't do more than drool through his shattered jaw. It wasn't until three-thirty in the morning that one Captain Davis, coming on duty, recognized the man as a retired flower salesman from the Bronx called Hank Vasarely. Hank, it seemed, was regularly arrested for threatening behavior and indecent exposure, all in the name of Jehovah. Appearances deceived: he was about as dangerous as the Easter Bunny. This was not the Subway Slaughterer. But by the time the cops had worked that out, Mahogany had been about his business a long while.

⁌

IT WAS ELEVEN-FIFTEEN WHEN KAUFMAN GOT on the Express through to Mott Avenue. He shared the car with two other travelers. One was a middle-aged black woman in a purple coat, the other a pale, acne-ridden adolescent who was staring at the "Kiss My White Ass" graffiti on the ceiling with spaced-out eyes.

Kaufman was in the first car. He had a journey of thirty-five minutes' duration ahead of him. He let his eyes slide closed, reassured by the rhythmical rocking of the train. It was a tedious journey and he was tired. He didn't see the lights flicker off in the second car. He didn't see Mahogany's face, either, staring through the door between the cars, looking through for some more meat.

44

At 14th Street the black woman got out. Nobody got in.

Kaufman opened his eyes briefly, taking in the empty platform at 14th, then shut them again. The doors hissed closed. He was drifting in that warm somewhere between alertness and sleep and there was a fluttering of nascent dreams in his head. It was a good feeling. The train was off again, rattling down into the tunnels.

Maybe, at the back of his dozing mind, Kaufman half-registered that the doors between the second and first cars had been slid open. Maybe he smelt the sudden gush of tunnel air, and registered that the noise of wheels was momentarily louder. But he chose to ignore it.

Maybe he even heard the scuffle as Mahogany subdued the youth with the spaced-out stare. But the sound was too distant and the promise of sleep was too tempting. He drowsed on.

For some reason his dreams were of his mother's kitchen. She was chopping turnips and smiling sweetly as she chopped. He was only small in his dream and was looking up at her radiant face while she worked. Chop. Chop. Chop.

His eyes jerked open. His mother vanished. The car was empty and the youth was gone.

How long had he been dozing? He hadn't remembered the train stopping at West 4th Street. He got up, his head full of slumber, and almost fell over as the train rocked violently. It seemed to have gathered quite a substantial head of speed. Maybe the driver was keen to be home, wrapped up in bed with his wife. They were going at a fair lick; in fact it was bloody terrifying.

There was a blind drawn down over the window between the cars which hadn't been down before as he remembered. A little concern crept into Kaufman's sober head. Suppose he'd been sleeping a long while, and the guard had overlooked him in the car. Perhaps they'd passed Far Rockaway and the train was now speeding on its way to wherever they took the trains for the night.

"Fuck it," he said aloud.

Should he go forward and ask the driver? It was such a bloody idiot question to ask: where am I? At this time of night was he likely to get more than a stream of abuse by way of reply?

Then the train began to slow.

A station. Yes, a station. The train emerged from the tunnel and into the dirty light of the station at West 4th Street. He'd missed no stops.

So where had the boy gone?

He'd either ignored the warning on the car wall forbidding transfer between the cars while in transit, or else he'd gone into the driver's cabin up front. Probably between the driver's legs even now, Kaufman thought, his lip curling. It wasn't unheard of. This was the Palace of Delights, after all, and everyone had their right to a little love in the dark.

Kaufman shrugged to himself. What did he care where the boy had gone?

The doors closed. Nobody had boarded the train. It shunted off from the station, the lights flickering as it used a surge of power to pick up some speed again.

Kaufman felt the desire for sleep come over him afresh, but the sudden fear of being lost had pumped adrenaline into his system, and his limbs were tingling with nervous energy.

His senses were sharpened too.

Even over the clatter and the rumble of the wheels on the tracks, he heard the sound of tearing cloth coming from the next car. Was someone tearing their shirt off?

He stood up, grasping one of the straps for balance.

The window between the cars was completely curtained off, but he stared at it, frowning, as though he might suddenly discover X-ray vision. The car rocked and rolled. It was really traveling again.

Another ripping sound.

Was it rape?

With no more than a mild voyeuristic urge he moved down the see-sawing car towards the intersecting door, hoping there might be a chink in the curtain. His eyes were still fixed on the window, and he failed to notice the splatters of blood he was treading in. Until—

—his heel slipped. He looked down. His stomach almost saw the blood before his brain and the ham on whole wheat was halfway up his gullet catching in the back of his throat. Blood. He took several large gulps of stale air and looked away—back at the window.

His head was saying: blood. Nothing would make the word go away.

There was no more than a yard or two between him and the door now. He had to look. There was blood on his shoe, and a thin trail to the next car, but he still had to look.

He had to.

He took two more steps to the door and scanned the curtain looking for a flaw in the blind: a pulled thread in the weave would be sufficient. There was a tiny hole. He glued his eye to it.

His mind refused to accept what his eyes were seeing beyond the door. It rejected the spectacle as preposterous, as a dreamed sight. His reason said it couldn't be real, but his flesh knew it was. His body became rigid with terror. His eyes, unblinking, could not close off the appalling scene through the curtain. He stayed at the door while the train rattled on, while his blood drained from his extremities, and his brain reeled from lack of oxygen. Bright spots of light flashed in front of his vision, blotting out the atrocity.

Then he fainted.

⌖

HE WAS UNCONSCIOUS WHEN THE TRAIN REACHED Jay Street. He was deaf to the driver's announcement that all travelers beyond that station would have to change

48

trains. Had he heard this he would have questioned the sense of it. No trains disgorged all their passengers at Jay Street; the line ran to Mott Avenue, via the Aqueduct Racetrack, past JFK Airport. He would have asked what kind of train this could be. Except that he already knew. The truth was hanging in the next car. It was smiling contentedly to itself from behind a bloody chain-mail apron.

This was the Midnight Meat Train.

⁂

THERE'S NO ACCOUNTING FOR TIME IN A DEAD faint. It could have been seconds or hours that passed before Kaufman's eyes flickered open again, and his mind focussed on his newfound situation.

He lay under one of the seats now, sprawled along the vibrating wall of the car, hidden from view. Fate was with him so far, he thought: somehow the rocking of the car must have jockeyed his unconscious body out of sight.

He thought of the horror in Car Two, and swallowed back vomit. He was alone. Wherever the guard was (murdered perhaps), there was no way he could call for help. And the driver? Was he dead at his controls? Was the train even now hurtling through an unknown tunnel, a tunnel without a single station to identify it, towards its destruction?

And if there was no crash to be killed in, there was

always the Butcher, still hacking away a door's thickness from where Kaufman lay.

Whichever way he turned, the name on the door was Death.

The noise was deafening, especially lying on the floor. Kaufman's teeth were shaking in their sockets and his face felt numb with the vibration; even his skull was aching.

Gradually he felt strength seeping back into his exhausted limbs. He cautiously stretched his fingers and clenched his fists, to set the blood flowing there again.

And as the feeling returned, so did the nausea. He kept seeing the grisly brutality of the next car. He'd seen photographs of murder victims before, of course, but these were no common murders. He was in the same train as the Subway Butcher, the monster who strung his victims up by the feet from the straps, hairless and naked.

How long would it be before the killer stepped through that door and claimed him? He was sure that if the slaughterer didn't finish him, expectation would.

He heard movement beyond the door.

Instinct took over. Kaufman thrust himself further under the seat and tucked himself up into a tiny ball, with his sick-white face to the wall. Then he covered his head with his hands and closed his eyes as tightly as any child in terror of the Bogeyman.

The door was slid open. Click. Whoosh. A rush of air up from the rails. It smelt stranger than any Kaufman had smelt before: and colder. This was somehow primal air in his nostrils, hostile and unfathomable air. It made him shudder.

The door closed. Click.

The Butcher was close, Kaufman knew it. He could be standing no more than a matter of inches from where he lay.

Was he even now looking down at Kaufman's back? Even now bending, knife in hand, to scoop Kaufman out of his hiding place, like a snail hooked from its shell?

Nothing happened. He felt no breath on his neck. His spine was not slit open.

There was simply a clatter of feet close to Kaufman's head; then that same sound receding.

Kaufman's breath, held in his lungs 'til they hurt, was expelled in a rasp between his teeth.

Mahogany was almost disappointed that the sleeping man had alighted at West 4th Street. He was hoping for one more job to do that night, to keep him occupied while they descended. But no: the man had gone. The potential victim hadn't looked that healthy anyway, he thought to himself, he was an anaemic Jewish accountant probably. The meat wouldn't have been of any quality. Mahogany walked the length of the car to the driver's cabin. He'd spend the rest of the journey there.

My Christ, thought Kaufman, he's going to kill the driver.

He heard the cabin door open. Then the voice of the Butcher: low and hoarse.

"Hi."

"Hi."

They knew each other.

"All done?"

"All done."

Kaufman was shocked by the banality of the exchange. All done? What did that mean: all done?

He missed the next few words as the train hit a particularly noisy section of track.

Kaufman could resist looking no longer. Warily he uncurled himself and glanced over his shoulder down the length of the car. All he could see was the Butcher's legs, and the bottom of the open cabin door. Damn. He wanted to see the monster's face again.

There was laughter now.

Kaufman calculated the risks of his situation: the mathematics of panic. If he remained where he was, sooner or later the Butcher would glance down at him, and he'd be mincemeat. On the other hand, if he were to move from his hiding place he would risk being seen and pursued. Which was worse: stasis, and meeting his death trapped in a hole; or making a break for it and confronting his Maker in the middle of the car?

Kaufman surprised himself with his mettle: he'd move.

Infinitesimally slowly he crawled out from under the seat, watching the Butcher's back every minute as he did so. Once out, he began to crawl towards the door. Each step he took was a torment, but the Butcher seemed far too engrossed in his conversation to turn around.

Kaufman had reached the door. He began to stand up, trying all the while to prepare himself for the sight he would meet in Car Two. The handle was grasped; and he slid the door open.

The noise of the rails increased, and a wave of dank air, stinking of nothing on earth, came up at him. Surely the Butcher must hear, or smell? Surely he must turn—

But no. Kaufman skinned his way through the slit he had opened and so through into the bloody chamber beyond.

Relief made him careless. He failed to latch the door properly behind him and it began to slide open with the buffeting of the train.

Mahogany put his head out of the cabin and stared down the car towards the door.

"What the fuck's that?" said the driver.

"Didn't close the door properly. That's all."

Kaufman heard the Butcher walking towards the door. He crouched, a ball of consternation, against the intersecting wall, suddenly aware of how full his bowels were. The door was pulled closed from the other side, and the footsteps receded again.

Safe, for another breath at least.

Kaufman opened his eyes, steeling himself for the slaughter pen in front of him.

There was no avoiding it.

It filled every one of his senses: the smell of opened entrails, the sight of the bodies, the feel of fluid on the floor under his fingers, the sound of the straps creaking beneath the weight of the corpses, even the air, tasting salty with blood. He was with death absolutely in that cubby-hole, hurtling through the dark.

But there was no nausea now. There was no feeling left but a casual revulsion. He even found himself peering at the bodies with some curiosity.

The carcass closest to him was the remains of the pimply youth he'd seen in Car One. The body hung upside-down, swinging back and forth to the rhythm of the train, in unison with its three fellows; an obscene danse macabre. Its arms dangled loosely from the shoulder joints, into which gashes an inch or two deep had been made, so the body would hang more neatly.

Every part of the dead kid's anatomy was swaying hypnotically. The tongue, hanging from the open mouth. The head, lolling on its slit neck. Even the youth's penis flapped from side to side on his plucked groin. The head wound and the open jugular still pulsed blood into a black bucket. There was an elegance about the whole sight: the sign of a job well-done.

Beyond that body were the strung-up corpses of two young white women and a darker-skinned male. Kaufman turned his head on one side to look at their faces. They were quite blank. One of the girls was a beauty. He decided the male had been Puerto Rican. All were shorn of their head and body hair. In fact the air was still pungent with the smell of the shearing. Kaufman slid up the wall out of the crouching position, and as he did so one of the women's bodies turned around, presenting a dorsal view.

He was not prepared for this last horror.

The meat of her back had been entirely cleft open from neck to buttock and the muscle had been peeled back to expose the glistening vertebrae. It was the final triumph of the Butcher's craft. Here they hung, these shaved, bled, slit slabs of humanity, opened up like fish, and ripe for devouring.

Kaufman almost smiled at the perfection of its horror. He felt an offer of insanity tickling the base of his skull, tempting him into oblivion, promising a blank indifference to the world.

He began to shake, uncontrollably. He felt his vocal cords trying to form a scream. It was intolerable: and yet to scream was to become in a short while like the creatures in front of him.

"Fuck it," he said, more loudly than he'd intended, then pushing himself off from the wall he began to walk down the car between the swaying corpses, observing the neat piles of clothes and belongings that sat on the seats beside their owners. Under his feet the floor was sticky with drying bile. Even with his eyes closed to cracks he could see the blood in the buckets too clearly: it was thick and heady, flecks of grit turning in it.

He was past the youth now and he could see the door into Car Three ahead. All he had to do was run this gauntlet of atrocities. He urged himself on, trying to ignore the horrors, and concentrate on the door that would lead him back into sanity.

He was past the first woman. A few more yards, he said to himself, ten steps at most, less if he walked with confidence.

Then the lights went out.

"Jesus Christ," he said.

The train lurched, and Kaufman lost his balance.

In the utter blackness he reached out for support and his flailing arms encompassed the body beside him. Before he could prevent himself he felt his hands sinking into the lukewarm flesh, and his fingers grasping the open edge of muscle on the dead woman's back, his fingertips touching the bone of her spine. His cheek was laid against the bald flesh of the thigh.

He screamed; and even as he screamed, the lights flickered back on.

And as they flickered back on, and his scream died, he heard the noise of the Butcher's feet approaching down the length of Car One towards the intervening door.

He let go of the body he was embracing. His face was smeared with blood from her leg. He could feel it on his cheek, like war paint.

The scream had cleared Kaufman's head and he suddenly felt released into a kind of strength. There would be no pursuit down the train, he knew that: there would be no cowardice, not now. This was going to be a primitive confrontation, two human beings, face-to-face. And there would be no trick—none—that he couldn't contemplate using to bring his enemy down. This was a matter of survival, pure and simple.

The door handle rattled.

Kaufman looked around for a weapon, his eye steady and calculating. His gaze fell on the pile of clothes beside the Puerto Rican's body. There was a knife there, lying amongst the rhinestone rings and the imitation gold chains. A long-bladed, immaculately clean weapon, probably the man's pride and joy. Reaching past the well-muscled body, Kaufman plucked the knife from the heap. It felt good in his hand; in fact it felt positively thrilling.

The door was opening, and the face of the slaughterer came into view.

Kaufman looked down the abattoir at Mahogany. He was not terribly fearsome, just another balding, overweight man of fifty. His face was heavy and his eyes deep-set. His mouth was rather small and delicately lipped. In fact he had a woman's mouth.

Mahogany could not understand where this intruder had appeared from, but he was aware that it was another oversight, another sign of increasing incompetence. He must dispatch this ragged creature immediately. After all

57

they could not be more than a mile or two from the end of the line. He must cut the little man down and have him hanging up by his heels before they reached their destination.

He moved into Car Two.

"You were asleep," he said, recognizing Kaufman. "I saw you."

Kaufman said nothing.

"You should have left the train. What were you trying to do? Hide from me?"

Kaufman still kept his silence.

Mahogany grasped the hand of the cleaver hanging from his well-used leather belt. It was dirty with blood, as were his chain-mail apron, his hammer and his saw.

"As it is," he said, "I'll have to do away with you."

Kaufman raised the knife. It looked a little small beside the Butcher's paraphernalia.

"Fuck it," he said.

Mahogany grinned at the little man's pretensions to defense.

"You shouldn't have seen this: it's not for the likes of you," he said, taking another step towards Kaufman. "It's secret."

Oh, so he's the divinely inspired type, is he? thought Kaufman. That explains something.

"Fuck it," he said again.

The Butcher frowned. He didn't like the little man's indifference to his work, to his reputation.

"We all have to die sometime," he said. "You should be well pleased: you're not going to be burnt up like most of them: I can use you. To feed the Fathers."

Kaufman's only response was a grin. He was past being terrorized by this gross, shambling hulk.

The Butcher unhooked the cleaver from his belt and brandished it.

"A dirty little Jew like you," he said, "should be thankful to be useful at all: meat's the best you can aspire to."

Without warning, the Butcher swung. The cleaver divided the air at some speed, but Kaufman stepped back. The cleaver sliced his coat arm and buried itself in the Puerto Rican's shank. The impact half-severed the leg and the weight of the body opened the gash even further. The exposed meat of the thigh was like prime steak, succulent and appetizing.

The Butcher started to drag the cleaver out of the wound, and in that moment Kaufman sprang. The knife sped towards Mahogany's eye, but an error of judgement buried it instead in his neck. It transfixed the column and appeared in a little gout of gore on the other side. Straight through. In one stroke. Straight through.

Mahogany felt the blade in his neck as a choking sensation, almost as though he had caught a chicken bone in his throat. He made a ridiculous, halfhearted coughing sound. Blood issued from his lips, painting them, like lipstick on his woman's mouth. The cleaver clattered to the floor.

Kaufman pulled out the knife. The two wounds spouted little arcs of blood.

Mahogany collapsed to his knees, staring at the knife that had killed him. The little man was watching him quite passively. He was saying something, but Mahogany's ears were deaf to the remarks, as though he were underwater.

Mahogany suddenly went blind. He knew with a nostalgia for his senses that he would not see or hear again. This was death: it was on him for certain.

His hands still felt the weave of his trousers, however, and the hot splashes on his skin. His life seemed to totter on its tiptoes while his fingers grasped at one last sense . . . then his body collapsed, and his hands, and his life, and his sacred duty folded up under a weight of grey flesh.

The Butcher was dead.

Kaufman dragged gulps of stale air into his lungs and grabbed one of the straps to steady his reeling body. Tears blotted out the shambles he stood in. A time passed: he didn't know how long; he was lost in a dream of victory.

Then the train began to slow. He felt and heard the brakes being applied. The hanging bodies lurched forward as the careering train slowed, its wheels squealing on rails that were sweating slime.

Curiosity overtook Kaufman.

Would the train shunt into the Butcher's underground slaughterhouse, decorated with the meats he had gathered through his career? And the laughing driver, so indifferent to the massacre, what would he do once the train had stopped? Whatever happened now was academic. He could face anything at all; watch and see.

The tannoy crackled. The voice of the driver:

"We're here, man. Better take your place, eh?"

Take your place? What did that mean?

The train had slowed to a snail's pace. Outside the windows, everything was as dark as ever. The lights flickered, then went out. This time they didn't come back on.

Kaufman was left in total darkness.

"We'll be out in half-an-hour," the tannoy announced, so like any station report.

The train had come to a stop. The sound of its wheels on the tracks, the rush of its passage, which Kaufman had grown so used to, were suddenly absent. All he could hear was the hum of the tannoy. He could still see nothing at all.

Then, a hiss. The doors were opening. A smell entered the car, a smell so caustic that Kaufman clapped his hand over his face to shut it out.

He stood in silence, hand to mouth, for what seemed a lifetime. See no evil. Hear no evil. Speak no evil.

Then, there was a flicker of light outside the window.

It threw the door frame into silhouette, and it grew stronger by degrees. Soon there was sufficient light in the car for Kaufman to see the crumpled body of the Butcher at his feet, and the sallow sides of meat hanging on every side of him.

There was a whisper too, from the dark outside the train, a gathering of tiny noises like the voices of beetles. In the tunnel, shuffling towards the train, were human beings. Kaufman could see their outlines now. Some of them carried torches, which burned with a dead brown light. The noise was perhaps their feet on the damp earth, or perhaps their tongues clicking, or both.

Kaufman wasn't as naive as he'd been an hour before. Could there be any doubt as to the intention these things had, coming out of the blackness towards the train? The Butcher had slaughtered the men and women as meat for these cannibals, they were coming, like diners at the dinner-gong, to eat in this restaurant car.

Kaufman bent down and picked up the cleaver the Butcher had dropped. The noise of the creatures' approach was louder every moment. He backed down the car away from the open doors, only to find that the doors behind him were also open, and there was the whisper of approach there too.

He shrank back against one of the seats, and was about to take refuge under it when a hand, thin and frail to the point of transparency, appeared around the door.

He could not look away. Not that terror froze him as it had at the window. He simply wanted to watch.

The creature stepped into the car. The torches behind it threw its face into shadow, but its outline could be clearly seen.

There was nothing very remarkable about it.

It had two arms and two legs as he did; its head was not abnormally shaped. The body was small, and the effort of climbing into the train made its breath coarse. It seemed more geriatric than psychotic; generations of fictional man-eaters had not prepared him for its distressing vulnerability.

Behind it, similar creatures were appearing out of the darkness, shuffling into the train. In fact they were coming in at every door.

Kaufman was trapped. He weighed the cleaver in his hands, getting the balance of it, ready for the battle with these antique monsters. A torch had been brought into the car, and it illuminated the faces of the leaders.

They were completely bald. The tired flesh of their faces was pulled tight over their skulls, so that it shone with tension. There were stains of decay and disease on their skin, and in places the muscle had withered to a black pus, through which the bone of cheek or temple was showing. Some of them were naked as babies, their pulpy, syphilitic bodies scarcely sexed. What had been breasts were leathery bags hanging off the torso, the genitalia shrunken away.

Worse sights than the naked amongst them were those who wore a veil of clothes. It soon dawned on Kaufman that the rotting fabric slung around their shoulders or knotted about their midriffs was made of human skins. Not one, but a dozen or more, heaped haphazardly on top of each other, like pathetic trophies.

The leaders of this grotesque meal-line had reached the bodies now, and the gracile hands were laid upon the shanks of meat, and were running up and down the shaved flesh in a manner that suggested sensual pleasure. Tongues were dancing out of mouths, flecks of spittle landing on the meat. The eyes of the monsters were flickering back and forth with hunger and excitement.

Eventually one of them saw Kaufman.

Its eyes stopped flickering for a moment, and fixed on him. A look of inquiry came over the face, making a parody of puzzlement.

"You," it said. The voice was as wasted as the lips it came from.

Kaufman raised the cleaver a little, calculating his chances. There were perhaps thirty of them in the car and many more outside. But they looked so weak, and they had no weapons but their skin and bones.

The monster spoke again, its voice quite well-modulated, when it found itself, the piping of a once-cultured, once-charming man.

"You came after the other, yes?"

It glanced down at the body of Mahogany. It had clearly taken in the situation very quickly.

"Old anyway," it said, its watery eyes back on Kaufman, studying him with care.

"Fuck you," said Kaufman.

The creature attempted a wry smile, but it had almost forgotten the technique and the result was a grimace which exposed a mouthful of teeth that had been systematically filed into points.

"You must now do this for us," it said through the bestial grin. "We cannot survive without food."

The hand patted the rump of human flesh. Kaufman had no reply to the idea. He just stared in disgust as the fingernails slid into the cleft in the buttocks, feeling the swell of tender muscle.

"It disgusts us no less than you," said the creature. "But we're bound to eat this meat, or we die. God knows, I have no appetite for it."

The thing was drooling nevertheless.

Kaufman found his voice. It was small, more with a confusion of feelings than with fear.

"What are you?" He remembered the bearded man in the Deli. "Are you accidents of some kind?"

"We are the City fathers," the thing said. "And mothers, and daughters and sons. The builders, the lawmakers. We made this city."

"New York?" said Kaufman. The Palace of Delights?

"Before you were born, before anyone living was born."

As it spoke the creature's fingernails were running up under the skin of the split body, and were peeling the thin elastic layer off the luscious brawn. Behind Kaufman, the other creatures had begun to unhook the bodies from the straps, their hands laid in that same delighting manner on the smooth breasts and flanks of flesh. These too had begun skinning the meat.

"You will bring us more," the father said. "More meat for us. The other one was weak."

Kaufman stared in disbelief.

"Me?" he said. "Feed you? What do you think I am?"

"You must do it for us, and for those older than us. For those born before the city was thought of, when America was a timberland and desert."

The fragile hand gestured out of the train.

Kaufman's gaze followed the pointing finger into the gloom. There was something else outside the train which he'd failed to see before; much bigger than anything human.

The pack of creatures parted to let Kaufman through so that he could inspect more closely whatever it was that stood outside, but his feet would not move.

"Go on," said the father.

Kaufman thought of the city he'd loved. Were these really its ancients, its philosophers, its creators? He had to believe it. Perhaps there were people on the surface—bureaucrats, politicians, authorities of every kind—who knew this horrible secret and whose lives were dedicated

66

to preserving these abominations, feeding them, as savages feed lambs to their gods. There was a horrible familiarity about this ritual. It rang a bell—not in Kaufman's conscious mind, but in his deeper, older self.

His feet, no longer obeying his mind, but his instinct to worship, moved. He walked through the corridor of bodies and stepped out of the train.

The light of the torches scarcely began to illuminate the limitless darkness outside. The air seemed solid, it was so thick with the smell of ancient earth. But Kaufman smelt nothing. His head bowed, it was all he could do to prevent himself from fainting again.

It was there; the precursor of man. The original American, whose homeland this was before the Passamaquoddy or Cheyenne. Its eyes, if it had eyes, were on him.

His body shook. His teeth chattered.

He could hear the noise of its anatomy: ticking, crackling, sobbing.

It shifted a little in the dark.

The sound of its movement was awesome. Like a mountain sitting up.

Kaufman's face was raised to it, and without thinking about what he was doing or why, he fell to his knees in the shit in front of the Father of Fathers.

Every day of his life had been leading to this day, every moment quickening to this incalculable moment of holy terror.

Had there been sufficient light in that pit to see the whole, perhaps his tepid heart would have burst. As it was he felt it flutter in his chest as he saw what he saw.

It was a giant. Without head or limb. Without a feature that was analogous to human, without an organ that made sense, or senses. If it was like anything, it was like a shoal of fish. A thousand snouts all moving in unison, budding, blossoming and withering rhythmically. It was iridescent, like mother-of-pearl, but it was sometimes deeper than any color Kaufman knew, or could put a name to.

That was all Kaufman could see, and it was more than he wanted to see. There was much more in the darkness, flickering and flapping.

But he could look no longer. He turned away. And as he did so a football was pitched out of the train and rolled to a halt in front of the Father.

At least he thought it was a football, until he peered more attentively at it, and recognized it as a human head, the head of the Butcher. The skin of the face had been peeled off in strips. It glistened with blood as it lay in front of its Lord.

Kaufman looked away, and walked back to the train. Every part of his body seemed to be weeping but his eyes. They were too hot with the sight behind him, they boiled his tears away.

Inside, the creatures had already set about their supper. One, he saw, was plucking the blue sweet morsel of a woman's eye out of the socket. Another had a hand in its mouth. At Kaufman's feet lay the Butcher's headless corpse, still bleeding profusely from where its neck had been bitten through.

The little father who had spoken earlier stood in front of Kaufman.

"Serve us?" it asked gently, as you might ask a cow to follow you.

Kaufman was staring at the cleaver, the Butcher's symbol of office. The creatures were leaving the car now, dragging the half-eaten bodies after them. As the torches were taken out of the car, darkness was returning.

But before the lights had completely disappeared the father reached out and took hold of Kaufman's face, thrusting him round to look at himself in the filthy glass of the car window.

It was a thin reflection, but Kaufman could see quite well enough how changed he was. Whiter than any living man should be, covered in grime and blood.

The father's hand still gripped Kaufman's face, and its forefinger hooked into his mouth and down his gullet, the nail scoring the back of his throat. Kaufman gagged on the intruder, but had no will left to repel the attack.

"Serve," said the creature. "In silence."

Too late, Kaufman realized the intention of the finger—

Suddenly his tongue was seized tight and twisted on the root. Kaufman, in shock, dropped the cleaver. He tried to scream, but no sound came. Blood was in his throat, he heard his flesh tearing, and agonies convulsed him.

Then the hand was out of his mouth and the scarlet, spittle-covered fingers were in front of his face, with his tongue held between thumb and forefinger.

Kaufman was speechless.

"Serve," said the father, and stuffed the tongue into his own mouth, chewing on it with evident satisfaction. Kaufman fell to his knees, spewing up his sandwich.

The father was already shuffling away into the dark; the rest of the ancients had disappeared into their warren for another night.

The tannoy crackled.

"Home," said the driver.

The doors hissed closed and the sound of power surged through the train. The lights flickered on, then off again, then on.

The train began to move.

Kaufman lay on the floor, tears pouring down his face, tears of discomfiture and of resignation. He would bleed to death, he decided, where he lay. It wouldn't matter if he died. It was a foul world anyway.

❖

THE DRIVER WOKE HIM. HE OPENED HIS EYES. The face that was looking down at him was black, and not unfriendly. It grinned. Kaufman tried to say something, but his mouth was sealed up with dried blood. He jerked his head around like a driveler trying to spit out a word. Nothing came but grunts.

He wasn't dead. He hadn't bled to death.

The driver pulled him to his knees, talking to him as though he were a three-year-old.

"You got a job to do, my man: they're very pleased with you."

The driver had licked his fingers, and was rubbing Kaufman's swollen lips, trying to part them.

"Lots to learn before tomorrow night . . ."

Lots to learn. Lots to learn.

He led Kaufman out of the train. They were in no station he had ever seen before. It was white-tiled and absolutely pristine; a station-keeper's Nirvana. No graffiti disfigured the walls. There were no token-booths, but then there were no gates and no passengers either. This was a line that provided only one service: the Meat Train.

A morning shift of cleaners was already busy hosing the blood off the seats and the floor of the train. Somebody was stripping the Butcher's body, in preparation for dispatch to New Jersey. All around Kaufman people were at work.

A rain of dawn light was pouring through a grating in the roof of the station. Motes of dust hung in the beams, turning over and over. Kaufman watched them, entranced.

He hadn't seen such a beautiful thing since he was a child. Lovely dust. Over and over, and over and over.

The driver had managed to separate Kaufman's lips. His mouth was too wounded for him to move it, but at least he could breathe easily. And the pain was already beginning to subside.

The driver smiled at him, then turned to the rest of the workers in the station.

"I'd like to introduce Mahogany's replacement. Our new butcher," he announced.

The workers looked at Kaufman. There was a certain deference in their faces, which he found appealing.

Kaufman looked up at the sunlight, now falling all around him. He jerked his head, signifying that he wanted to go up, into the open air. The driver nodded, and led him up a steep flight of steps and through an alleyway and so out onto the sidewalk.

It was a beautiful day. The bright sky over New York was streaked with filaments of pale pink cloud, and the air smelt of morning.

The Streets and Avenues were practically empty. At a distance an occasional cab crossed an intersection, its engine a whisper; a runner sweated past on the other side of the street.

Very soon these same deserted sidewalks would be thronged with people. The city would go about its business in ignorance: never knowing what it was built upon, or what it owed its life to. Without hesitation,

Kaufman fell to his knees and kissed the dirty concrete with his bloody lips, silently swearing his eternal loyalty to its continuance.

The Palace of Delights received the adoration without comment.

THE YATTERING

AND JACK

WHY THE POWERS (LONG MAY THEY HOLD court; long may they shit light on the heads of the damned) had sent it out from Hell to stalk Jack Polo, the Yattering couldn't discover. Whenever he passed a tentative inquiry along the system to his master, just asking the simple question "What am I doing here?" it was answered with a swift rebuke for its curiosity. None of its business, came the reply, its business was to do. Or die trying. And after six months of pursuing Polo, the Yattering was beginning to see extinction as an easy option. This endless game of hide-and-seek was to nobody's benefit, and the Yattering's immense frustration.

It feared ulcers, it feared psychosomatic leprosy (condition lower demons like itself were susceptible to), worst of all it feared losing its temper completely and killing the man outright in an uncontrollable fit of pique.

What was Jack Polo anyway?

A gherkin importer; by the balls of Leviticus, he was simply a gherkin importer. His life was worn out, his family was dull, his politics were simple-minded and his theology nonexistent. The man was a no-account, one of nature's blankest little numbers—why bother with the likes of him? This wasn't a Faust: a pact-maker, a soul-seller. This one wouldn't look twice at the chance of divine inspiration: he'd sniff, shrug and get on with his gherkin importing.

Yet the Yattering was bound to that house, long night and longer day, until he had the man a lunatic, or as good as. It was going to be a lengthy job, if not interminable. Yes, there were times when even psychosomatic leprosy would be bearable if it meant being invalided off this impossible mission.

For his part, Jack J. Polo continued to be the most unknowing of men. He had always been that way; indeed his history was littered with the victims of his naïveté. When his late, lamented wife had cheated on him (he'd been in the house on at least two of the occasions, watching the television) he was the last one to find out. And the clues they'd left behind them! A blind, deaf and dumb man would have become suspicious. Not Jack. He pottered about his dull business and never noticed the tang of the adulterer's cologne, nor the abnormal regularity with which his wife changed the bed-linen.

He was no less disinterested in events when his younger daughter, Amanda, confessed her lesbianism to him. His response was a sigh and a puzzled look.

"Well, as long as you don't get pregnant, darling," he replied, and sauntered off into the garden, blithe as ever.

What chance did a fury have with a man like that?

To a creature trained to put its meddling fingers into the wounds of the human psyche, Polo offered a surface so glacial, so utterly without distinguishing marks, as to deny malice any hold whatsoever.

Events seemed to make no dent in his perfect indifference. His life's disasters seemed not to scar his mind at all. When, eventually, he was confronted with the truth about his wife's infidelity (he found them screwing in the bath) he couldn't bring himself to be hurt or humiliated.

"These things happen," he said to himself, backing out of the bathroom to let them finish what they'd started.

"Che sera, sera."

Che sera, sera. The man muttered that damn phrase with monotonous regularity. He seemed to live by that philosophy of fatalism, letting attacks on his manhood, ambition and dignity slide off his ego like rainwater from his bald head.

The Yattering had heard Polo's wife confess all to her

husband (it was hanging upside down from the light-fitting, invisible as ever) and the scene had made it wince. There was the distraught sinner, begging to be accused, bawled at, struck even, and instead of giving her the satisfaction of his hatred, Polo had just shrugged and let her say her piece without a word of interruption, until she had no more to unbosom. She'd left, at length, more out of frustration and sorrow than guilt; the Yattering had heard her tell the bathroom mirror how insulted she was at her husband's lack of righteous anger. A little while after she'd flung herself off the balcony of the Roxy Cinema.

Her suicide was in some ways convenient for the fury. With the wife gone, and the daughters away from home, it could plan for more elaborate tricks to unnerve its victim, without ever having to concern itself with revealing its presence to creatures the powers had not marked for attack.

But the absence of the wife left the house empty during the days, and that soon became a burden of boredom the Yattering found scarcely supportable. The hours from nine to five, alone in the house, often seemed endless. It would mope and wander, planning bizarre and impractical revenges upon the Polo-man, pacing the rooms, heartsick, companioned only by the clicks and whirrs of the house as the radiators cooled, or the refrigerator switched itself on and off. The situation rapidly became so desperate that the arrival of the midday post became the high-point of the day, and an unshakeable melancholy would settle on the Yattering if the postman had nothing to deliver and passed by to the next house.

When Jack returned the games would begin in earnest. The usual warm-up routine: it would meet Jack at the door and prevent his key from turning in the lock. The contest would go on for a minute or two until Jack accidentally found the measure of the Yattering's resistance, and won the day. Once inside, it would start all the lampshades swinging. The man would usually ignore this performance, however violent the motion. Perhaps he might shrug and murmur: "Subsidence," under his breath, then, inevitably, *"Che sera, sera."*

In the bathroom, the Yattering would have squeezed toothpaste around the toilet seat and have plugged up the shower-head with soggy toilet paper. It would even share the shower with Jack, hanging unseen from the rail that held up the shower curtain and murmuring obscene suggestions in his ear. That was always successful, the demons were taught at the Academy. The obscenities in the ear routine never failed to distress clients, making them think they were conceiving of these pernicious acts themselves, and driving them to self-disgust, then to self-rejection and finally to madness. Of course, in a few cases the victims would be so inflamed by these whispered suggestions they'd go out on the streets and act upon them. Under such circumstances the victim would often

81

be arrested and incarcerated. Prison would lead to further crimes, and a slow dwindling of moral reserves— and the victory was won by that route. One way or another insanity would win out.

Except that for some reason this rule did not apply to Polo; he was unperturbable: a tower of propriety.

Indeed, the way things were going the Yattering would be the one to break. It was tired; so very tired. Endless days of tormenting the cat, reading the funnies in yesterday's newspaper, watching the game shows: they drained the fury. Lately, it had developed a passion for the woman who lived across the street from Polo. She was a young widow; and seemed to spend most of her life parading around the house stark naked. It was almost unbearable sometimes, in the middle of a day when the postman failed to call, watching the woman and knowing it could never cross the threshold of Polo's house.

This was the Law. The Yattering was a minor demon, and his soul-catching was strictly confined to the perimeters of his victim's house. To step outside was to relinquish all powers over the victim: to put itself at the mercy of humanity.

All June, all July and most of August it sweated in its prison, and all through those bright, hot months Jack Polo maintained complete indifference to the Yattering's attacks.

It was deeply embarrassing, and it was gradually destroying the demon's self-confidence, seeing this bland victim survive every trial and trick attempted upon him.

The Yattering wept.

The Yattering screamed.

In a fit of uncontrollable anguish, it boiled the water in the aquarium, poaching the guppies.

Polo heard nothing. Saw nothing.

⁜

AT LAST, IN LATE SEPTEMBER, THE YATTERING broke one of the first rules of its condition, and appealed directly to its masters.

Autumn is Hell's season; and the demons of the higher dominations were feeling benign. They condescended to speak to their creature.

"What do you want?" asked Beelzebub, his voice blackening the air in the lounge.

"This man . . ." the Yattering began nervously.

"Yes?"

"This Polo . . ."

"Yes?"

"I am without issue upon him. I can't get panic upon him, I can't breed fear or even mild concern upon him. I am sterile, Lord of the Flies, and I wish to be put out of my misery."

For a moment Beelzebub's face formed in the mirror over the mantelpiece.

"You want *what*?"

Beelzebub was part elephant, part wasp. The Yattering was terrified.

"I—want to die."

"You cannot die."

"From this world. Just die from this world. Fade away. Be replaced."

"You will not die."

"But I can't break him!" the Yattering shrieked, tearful.

"You must."

"Why?"

"Because we tell you to." Beelzebub always used the royal "we," though unqualified to do so.

"Let me at least know why I'm in this house," the Yattering appealed. "What is he? Nothing! He's nothing!"

Beelzebub found this rich. He laughed, buzzed, trumpeted.

"Jack Johnson Polo is the child of a worshipper at the Church of Lost Salvation. He belongs to us."

"But why should you want him? He's so dull."

"We want him because his soul was promised to us, and his mother did not deliver it. Or herself come to that. She cheated us. She died in the arms of a priest, and was safely escorted to—"

The word that followed was anathema. The Lord of the Flies could barely bring himself to pronounce it.

"—Heaven," said Beelzebub, with infinite loss in his voice.

"Heaven," said the Yattering, not knowing quite what was meant by the word.

"Polo is to be hounded in the name of the Old One, and punished for his mother's crimes. No torment is too profound for a family that has cheated us."

"I'm tired," the Yattering pleaded, daring to approach the mirror. "Please. I beg you."

"Claim this man," said Beelzebub, "or you will suffer in his place."

The figure in the mirror waved its black and yellow trunk and faded.

"Where is your pride?" said the master's voice as it shriveled into the distance. "Pride, Yattering, pride."

Then he was gone.

In its frustration the Yattering picked up the cat and threw it into the fire, where it was rapidly cremated. If only the law allowed such easy cruelty to be visited upon human flesh, it thought. If only. If only. Then it'd make Polo suffer such torments. But no. The Yattering knew the laws as well as the back of its hand; they had been flayed onto its exposed cortex as a fledgling demon by its teachers. And Law One stated: "Thou shalt not lay palm upon thy victims."

It had never been told why this law pertained, but it did.

"Thou shalt not . . ."

So the whole painful process continued. Day in, day out, and still the man showed no sign of yielding. Over the next few weeks the Yattering killed two more cats that Polo brought home to replace his treasured Freddy (now ash).

The first of these poor victims was drowned in the toilet bowl one idle Friday afternoon. It was a petty satisfaction to see the look of distaste register on Polo's face as he unzipped his fly and glanced down. But any pleasure the Yattering took in Jack's discomfiture was canceled out by the blithely efficient way in which the man dealt with the dead cat, hoisting the bundle of soaking fur out of the pan, wrapping it in a towel and burying it in the back garden with scarcely a murmur.

The third cat that Polo brought home was wise to the invisible presence of the demon from the start. There was indeed an entertaining week in mid-November when life for the Yattering became almost interesting while it played cat and mouse with Freddy the Third. Freddy played the mouse. Cats not being especially bright animals, the game was scarcely a great intellectual challenge, but it made for a change from the endless days of waiting, haunting and failing. At least the creature accepted the Yattering's presence. Eventually however, in a filthy mood (caused by the remarriage of the Yattering's naked widow) the demon lost its temper with the cat. It was sharpening its nails on the nylon carpet, clawing and scratching at the pile for hours on end. The noise put the demon's metaphysical teeth on edge. It looked at the cat once, briefly, and it flew apart as though it had swallowed a live grenade.

The effect was spectacular. The results were gross. Cat-brain, cat-fur, cat-gut everywhere.

Polo got home that evening exhausted, and stood in the doorway of the dining-room, his face sickened, surveying the carnage that had been Freddy III.

"Damn dogs," he said. "Damn, damn dogs."

There was anger in his voice. Yes, exulted the Yattering, anger. The man was upset: there was clear evidence of emotion on his face.

Elated, the demon raced through the house, determined to capitalize on its victory. It opened and slammed every door. It smashed vases. It set the lampshades swinging.

Polo just cleaned up the cat.

The Yattering threw itself downstairs, tore up a pillow. Impersonated a thing with a limp and an appetite for human flesh in the attic, and giggled.

Polo just buried Freddy III, beside the grave of Freddy II, and the ashes of Freddy I.

Then he retired to bed, without his pillow.

The demon was utterly stumped. If the man could not raise more than a flicker of concern when his cat was exploded in the dining-room, what chance had it got of ever breaking the bastard?

There was one last opportunity left.

It was approaching Christ's Mass, and Jack's children would be coming home to the bosom of the family.

Perhaps they could convince him that all was not well with the world; perhaps they could get their fingernails under his flawless indifference, and begin to break him down. Hoping against hope, the Yattering sat out the weeks to late December, planning its attacks with all the imaginative malice it could muster.

Meanwhile, Jack's life sauntered on. He seemed to live apart from his experience, living his life as an author might write a preposterous story, never involving himself in the narrative too deeply. In several significant ways, however, he showed his enthusiasm for the coming holiday. He cleared his daughters' rooms immaculately. He made their beds up with sweet-smelling linen. He cleaned every speck of cat's blood out of the carpet. He even set up a Christmas tree in the lounge, hung with iridescent balls, tinsel and presents.

Once in a while, as he went about the preparations, Jack thought of the game he was playing, and quietly calculated the odds against him. In the days to come he would have to measure not only his own suffering, but that of his daughters, against the possible victory. And always, when he made these calculations, the chance of victory seemed to outweigh the risks.

So he continued to write his life, and waited.

Snow came, soft pats of it against the windows, against the door. Children arrived to sing carols, and he was generous to them. It was possible, for a brief time, to believe in peace on earth.

Late in the evening of the twenty-third of December the daughters arrived, in a flurry of cases and kisses. The youngest, Amanda, arrived home first. From its vantage point on the landing the Yattering viewed the young woman balefully. She didn't look like ideal material in which to induce a breakdown. In fact, she looked dangerous. Gina followed an hour or two later; a smoothly polished woman of the world at twenty-four, she looked every bit as intimidating as her sister. They came into the house with their bustle and their laughter; they rearranged the furniture; they threw out the junkfood in the freezer; they told each other (and their father) how much they had missed each other's company. Within the space of a few hours the drab house was repainted with light, and fun and love.

It made the Yattering sick.

Whimpering, it hid its head in the bedroom to block out the din of affection, but the shock-waves enveloped it. All it could do was sit, and listen, and refine its revenge.

Jack was pleased to have his beauties home. Amanda so full of opinions, and so strong, like her mother. Gina more like *his* mother: poised, perceptive. He was so happy in their presence he could have wept; and here was he, the proud father, putting them both at such risk. But what was the alternative? If he had canceled the Christmas celebrations, it would have looked highly suspicious. It might even have spoiled his whole strategy, wakening the enemy to the trick that was being played.

No; he must sit tight. Play dumb, the way the enemy had come to expect him to be.

The time would come for action.

At three-fifteen a.m. on Christmas morning the Yattering opened hostilities by throwing Amanda out of bed. A paltry performance at best, but it had the intended effect. Sleepily rubbing her bruised head, she climbed back into bed, only to have the bed buck and shake and fling her off again like an unbroken colt.

The noise woke the rest of the house. Gina was first in her sister's room.

"What's going on?"

"There's somebody under the bed."

"What?"

Gina picked up a paperweight from the dresser and demanded the assailant come out. The Yattering, invisible, sat on the windowseat and made obscene gestures at the women, tying knots in its genitalia.

Gina peered under the bed. The Yattering was clinging to the light fixture now, persuading it to swing backwards and forwards, making the room reel.

"There's nothing there—"

"There is."

Amanda knew. Oh yes, she knew.

"There's something here, Gina," she said. "Something in the room with us, I'm sure of it."

"No." Gina was absolute. "It's empty."

Amanda was searching behind the wardrobe when Polo came in.

"What's all the din?"

"There's something in the house, Daddy. I was thrown out of bed."

Jack looked at the crumpled sheets, the dislodged mattress, then at Amanda. This was the first test: he must lie as casually as possible.

"Looks like you've been having nightmares, beauty," he said, affecting an innocent smile.

"There was something under the bed," Amanda insisted.

"There's nobody here now."

"But I felt it."

"Well, I'll check the rest of the house," he offered, without enthusiasm for the task. "You two stay here, just in case."

As Polo left the room, the Yattering rocked the light a little more.

"Subsidence," said Gina.

It was cold downstairs, and Polo could have done without padding around barefoot on the kitchen tiles, but he was quietly satisfied that the battle had been joined in such a petty manner. He'd half-feared that the enemy would turn savage with such tender victims at hand. But no: he'd judged the mind of the creature quite accurately. It was one of the lower orders. Powerful, but slow. Capable of being inveigled beyond the limits

91

of its control. Carefully does it, he told himself, carefully does it.

He traipsed through the entire house, dutifully opening cupboards and peering behind the furniture, then returned to his daughters, who were sitting at the top of the stairs. Amanda looked small and pale, not the twenty-two-year-old woman she was, but a child again.

"Nothing doing," he told her with a smile. "It's Christmas morning and all through the house—"

Gina finished the rhyme.

"Nothing is stirring, not even a mouse."

"Not even a mouse, beauty."

At that moment the Yattering took its cue to fling a vase off the lounge mantelpiece.

Even Jack jumped.

"Shit," he said. He needed some sleep, but quite clearly the Yattering had no intention of letting them alone just yet.

"Che sera, sera," he murmured, scooping up the pieces of the Chinese vase, and putting them in a piece of newspaper. "The house is sinking a little on the left side, you know," he said more loudly. "It has been for years."

"Subsidence," said Amanda with quiet certainty, "would not throw me out of my bed."

Gina said nothing. The options were limited. The alternatives unattractive.

"Well maybe it was Santa Claus," said Polo, attempting

levity. He parceled up the pieces of the vase and wandered through into the kitchen, certain that he was being shadowed every step of the way. "What else can it be?" He threw the question over his shoulder as he stuffed the newspaper into the wastebin. "The only other explanation—" Here he became almost elated by his skimming so close to the truth. "The only other possible explanation is too preposterous for words."

It was an exquisite irony, denying the existence of the invisible world in the full knowledge that even now it breathed vengefully down his neck.

"You mean poltergeist?" said Gina.

"I mean anything that goes bang in the night. But, we're grown-up people, aren't we? We don't believe in Bogeymen."

"No," said Gina flatly, "I don't, but I don't believe the house is subsiding either."

"Well, it'll have to do for now," said Jack with nonchalant finality. "Christmas starts here. We don't want to spoil it talking about gremlins, now, do we?"

They laughed together.

Gremlins. That surely bit deep. To call the Hell-spawn a gremlin.

The Yattering, weak with frustration, acid tears boiling on its intangible cheeks, ground its teeth and kept its peace.

There would be time yet to beat the atheistic smile off

Jack Polo's smooth, fat face. Time aplenty. No half-measures from now on. No subtlety. It would be an all-out attack.

Let there be blood. Let there be agony.

They'd all break.

⁎

AMANDA WAS IN THE KITCHEN, PREPARING Christmas dinner, when the Yattering mounted its next attack. Through the house drifted the sound of King's College Choir, "O little town of Bethlehem, how still we see thee lie . . ."

The presents had been opened, the G and T's were being downed, the house was one warm embrace from roof to cellar.

In the kitchen a sudden chill permeated the heat and the steam, making Amanda shiver; she crossed to the window, which was ajar to clear the air, and closed it. Maybe she was catching something.

The Yattering watched her back as she busied herself about the kitchen, enjoying the domesticity for a day. Amanda felt the stare quite clearly. She turned round. Nobody, nothing. She continued to wash the Brussels sprouts, cutting into one with a worm curled in the middle. She drowned it.

The Choir sang on.

In the lounge, Jack was laughing with Gina about something.

Then, a noise. A rattling at first, followed by a beating of somebody's fists against a door. Amanda dropped the knife into the bowl of sprouts, and turned from the sink, following the sound. It was getting louder all the time. Like something locked in one of the cupboards, desperate to escape. A cat caught in the box, or a—

Bird.

It was coming from the oven.

Amanda's stomach turned, as she began to imagine the worst. Had she locked something in the oven when she'd put in the turkey? She called for her father, as she snatched up the oven cloth and stepped towards the cooker, which was rocking with the panic of its prisoner. She had visions of a basted cat leaping out at her, its fur burned off, its flesh half-cooked.

Jack was at the kitchen door.

"There's something in the oven," she said to him, as though he needed telling. The cooker was in a frenzy; its thrashing contents had all but beaten off the door.

He took the oven cloth from her. This is a new one, he thought. You're better than I judged you to be. This is clever. This is original.

Gina was in the kitchen now.

"What's cooking?" she quipped.

But the joke was lost as the cooker began to dance,

and the pans of boiling water were twitched off the burners onto the floor. Scalding water seared Jack's leg. He yelled, stumbling back into Gina, before diving at the cooker with a yell that wouldn't have shamed a Samurai.

The oven handle was slippery with heat and grease, but he seized it and flung the door down.

A wave of steam and blistering heat rolled out of the oven, smelling of succulent turkey-fat. But the bird inside had apparently no intentions of being eaten. It was flinging itself from side to side on the roasting tray, tossing gouts of gravy in all directions. Its crisp brown wings pitifully flailed and flapped, its legs beat a tattoo on the roof of the oven.

Then it seemed to sense the open door. Its wings stretched themselves out to either side of its stuffed bulk and it half hopped, half fell onto the oven door, in a mockery of its living self. Headless, oozing stuffing and onions, it flopped around as though nobody had told the damn thing it was dead, while the fat still bubbled on its bacon-strewn back.

Amanda screamed.

Jack dived for the door as the bird lurched into the air, blind but vengeful. What it intended to do once it reached its three cowering victims was never discovered. Gina dragged Amanda into the hallway with her father in hot pursuit, and the door was slammed closed as the blind bird flung itself against the panelling, beating on it with all its strength. Gravy seeped through the gap at the bottom of the door, dark and fatty.

The door had no lock, but Jack reasoned that the bird was not capable of turning the handle. As he backed away, breathless, he cursed his confidence. The opposition had more up its sleeve than he'd guessed.

Amanda was leaning against the wall sobbing, her face stained with splotches of turkey grease. All she seemed able to do was deny what she'd seen, shaking her head and repeating the word "no" like a talisman against the ridiculous horror that was still throwing itself against the door. Jack escorted her through to the lounge. The radio was still crooning carols which blotted out the din of the bird, but their promise of goodwill seemed small comfort.

Gina poured a hefty brandy for her sister and sat beside her on the sofa, plying her with spirits and reassurance in about equal measure. They made little impression on Amanda.

"What *was* that?" Gina asked her father, in a tone that demanded an answer.

"I don't know what it was," Jack replied.

"Mass hysteria?" Gina's displeasure was plain. Her father had a secret: he knew what was going on in the house, but he was refusing to cough up for some reason.

"What do I call: the Police or an exorcist?"

"Neither."

"For God's sake—"

"There's *nothing* going on, Gina. Really."

Her father turned from the window and looked at her. His eyes spoke what his mouth refused to say, that this was war.

Jack was afraid.

The house was suddenly a prison. The game was suddenly lethal. The enemy, instead of playing foolish games, meant harm, real harm to them all.

In the kitchen the turkey had at last conceded defeat. The carols on the radio had withered into a sermon on God's benedictions.

What had been sweet was sour and dangerous. He looked across the room at Amanda and Gina. Both, for their own reasons, were trembling. Polo wanted to tell them, wanted to explain what was going on. But the thing must be there, he knew, gloating.

He was wrong. The Yattering had retired to the attic, well-satisfied with its endeavours. The bird, it felt, had been a stroke of genius. Now it could rest a while: recuperate. Let the enemy's nerves tatter themselves in anticipation. Then, in its own good time, it would deliver the coup de grâce.

Idly, it wondered if any of the inspectors had seen his work with the turkey. Maybe they would be impressed enough by the Yattering's originality to improve its job-prospects. Surely it hadn't gone through all those years of training simply to chase half-witted imbeciles like Polo. There must be something more challenging available than that. It felt victory in its invisible bones: and it was a good feeling.

The pursuit of Polo would surely gain momentum now. His daughters would convince him (if he wasn't now quite convinced) that there was something terrible afoot. He would crack. He would crumble. Maybe he'd go classically mad: tear out his hair, rip off his clothes; smear himself with his own excrement.

Oh yes, victory was close. And wouldn't its masters be loving then? Wouldn't it be showered with praise, and power?

One more manifestation was all that was required. One final, inspired intervention, and Polo would be so much blubbering flesh.

Tired, but confident, the Yattering descended into the lounge.

Amanda was lying full-length on the sofa, asleep. She was obviously dreaming about the turkey. Her eyes rolled beneath her gossamer lids, her lower lip trembled. Gina sat beside the radio, which was silenced now. She had a book open on her lap, but she wasn't reading it.

The gherkin importer wasn't in the room. Wasn't that his footstep on the stair? Yes, he was going upstairs to relieve his brandy-full bladder.

Ideal timing.

The Yattering crossed the room. In her sleep Amanda

dreamt something dark flitting across her vision, something malign, something that tasted bitter in her mouth.

Gina looked up from her book.

The silver balls on the tree were rocking, gently. Not just the balls. The tinsel and the branches too.

In fact, the tree. The whole tree was rocking as though someone had just seized hold of it.

Gina had a very bad feeling about this. She stood up. The book slid to the floor.

The tree began to spin.

"Christ," she said. "Jesus Christ."

Amanda slept on.

The tree picked up momentum.

Gina walked as steadily as she could across to the sofa and tried to shake her sister awake. Amanda, locked in her dreams, resisted for a moment.

"Father," said Gina. Her voice was strong, and carried through into the hall. It also woke Amanda.

Downstairs, Polo heard a noise like a whining dog. No, like two whining dogs. As he ran down the stairs, the duet became a trio. He burst into the lounge half expecting all the hosts of Hell to be in there, dog-headed, dancing on his beauties.

But no. It was the Christmas tree that was whining, whining like a pack of dogs, as it spun and spun.

The lights had long since been pulled from their sockets. The air stank of singed plastic and pine-sap. The tree itself was spinning like a top, flinging decorations and presents off its tortured branches with the largesse of a mad king.

Jack tore his eyes from the spectacle of the tree and found Gina and Amanda crouching, terrified, behind the sofa.

"Get out of here," he yelled.

Even as he spoke, the television sat up impertinently on one leg and began to spin like the tree, gathering momentum quickly. The clock on the mantelpiece joined the pirouetting. The pokers beside the fire. The cushions. The ornaments. Each object added its own singular note to the orchestration of whines which were building up, second by second, to a deafening pitch. The air began to brim with the smell of burning wood, as friction heated the spinning tops to flash-point. Smoke swirled across the room.

Gina had Amanda by the arm, and was dragging her towards the door, shielding her face against the hail of pine-needles that the still-accelerating tree was throwing off.

Now the lights were spinning.

The books, having flung themselves off the shelves, had joined the tarantella.

Jack could see the enemy, in his mind's eye, racing between the objects like a juggler spinning plates on sticks, trying to keep them all moving at once. It must be exhausting work, he thought. The demon was probably close to collapse. It couldn't be thinking straight. Over-excited. Impulsive. Vulnerable. This must be the moment, if ever there was a moment, to join battle at last. To face the thing, defy it and trap it.

For its part, the Yattering was enjoying this orgy of destruction. It flung every movable object into the fray, setting everything spinning.

It watched with satisfaction as the daughters twitched and scurried; it laughed to see the old man stare, pop-eyed, at this preposterous ballet.

Surely he was nearly mad, wasn't he?

The beauties had reached the door, their hair and skin full of needles. Polo didn't see them leave. He ran across the room, dodging a rain of ornaments to do so, and picked up a brass toasting fork which the enemy had overlooked. Bric-a-brac filled the air around his head, dancing around with sickening speed. His flesh was bruised and punctured. But the exhilaration of joining battle had overtaken him, and he set about beating the books, and the clocks, and the china to smithereens. Like a man in a cloud of locusts he ran around the room, bringing down his favorite books in a welter of fluttering pages, smashing whirling Dresden, shattering the lamps. A litter of broken possessions swamped the floor, some of it still twitching as the life went out of the fragments. But for every object brought low, there were a dozen still spinning, still whining.

He could hear Gina at the door, yelling to him to get out, to leave it alone.

But it was so enjoyable, playing against the enemy more directly than he'd ever allowed himself before. He didn't want to give up. He wanted the demon to show itself, to be known, to be recognized.

He wanted confrontation with the Old One's emissary once and for all.

Without warning the tree gave way to the dictates of centrifugal force, and exploded. The noise was like a howl of death. Branches, twigs, needles, balls, lights, wire, ribbons, flew across the room. Jack, his back to the explosion, felt a gust of energy hit him hard, and he was flung to the ground. The back of his neck and his scalp were shot full of pine-needles. A branch, naked of greenery, shot past his head and impaled the sofa. Fragments of tree pattered to the carpet around him.

Now other objects around the room, spun beyond the tolerance of their structures, were exploding like the tree. The television blew up, sending a lethal wave of glass across the room, much of which buried itself in the opposite wall. Fragments of the television's innards, so hot they singed the skin, fell on Jack, as he elbowed himself towards the door like a soldier under bombardment.

The room was so thick with a barrage of shards it was like a fog. The cushions had lent their down to the scene, snowing on the carpet. Porcelain pieces—a beautifully glazed arm, a courtesan's head—bounced on the floor in front of his nose.

Gina was crouching at the door, urging him to hurry, her eyes narrowed against the hail. As Jack reached the door, and felt her arms around him, he swore he could hear laughter from the lounge. Tangible, audible laughter, rich and satisfied.

Amanda was standing in the hall, her hair full of pine-needles, staring down at him. He pulled his legs through the doorway and Gina slammed the door shut on the demolition.

"What is it?" she demanded. "Poltergeist? Ghost? Mother's ghost?"

The thought of his dead wife being responsible for such wholesale destruction struck Jack as funny.

Amanda was half smiling. Good, he thought, she's coming out of it. Then he met the vacant look in her eyes and the truth dawned. She'd broken, her sanity had taken refuge where this fantastique couldn't get at it.

"What's in there?" Gina was asking, her grip on his arm so strong it stopped the blood.

"I don't know," he lied. "Amanda?"

Amanda's smile didn't decay. She just stared on at him, through him.

"You do know."

"No."

"You're lying."

"I think . . ."

He picked himself off the floor, brushing the pieces of porcelain, the feathers, the glass, off his shirt and trousers.

"I think . . . I shall go for a walk."

Behind him, in the lounge, the last vestiges of whining had stopped. The air in the hallway was electric with unseen presences. It was very close to him, invisible as ever, but so close. This was the most dangerous time. He mustn't lose his nerve now. He must stand up as though nothing had happened; he must leave Amanda be, leave explanations and recriminations until it was all over and done with.

"Walk?" Gina said, disbelievingly.

"Yes . . . walk . . . I need some fresh air."

"You can't leave us here."

"I'll find somebody to help us clear up."

"But Mandy."

"She'll get over it. Leave her be."

That was hard. That was almost unforgivable. But it was said now.

He walked unsteadily towards the front door, feeling nauseous after so much spinning. At his back Gina was raging.

"You just can't leave! Are you out of your mind?"

"I need the air," he said, as casually as his thumping heart and his parched throat would permit. "So I'll just go out for a moment."

No, the Yattering said. No, no, no.

It was behind him, Polo could feel it. So angry now, so ready to twist off his head. Except that it wasn't allowed *ever* to touch him. But he could feel its resentment like a physical presence.

He took another step towards the front door.

It was with him still, dogging his every step. His shadow, his fetch; unshakeable. Gina shrieked at him, "You sonofabitch, look at Mandy! She's lost her mind!"

No, he mustn't look at Mandy. If he looked at Mandy he might weep, he might break down as the thing wanted him to, then everything would be lost.

"She'll be all right," he said, barely above a whisper.

He reached for the front door handle. The demon bolted the door, quickly, loudly. No temper left for pretense now.

Jack, keeping his movements as even as possible, unbolted the door, top and bottom. It bolted again.

It was thrilling, this game; it was also terrifying. If he pushed too far surely the demon's frustration would override its lessons?

Gently, smoothly, he unbolted the door again. Just as gently, just as smoothly, the Yattering bolted it.

Jack wondered how long he could keep this up for. Somehow he had to get outside: he had to coax it over the threshold. One step was all that the law required, according to his researches. One simple step.

Unbolted. Bolted. Unbolted. Bolted.

Gina was standing two or three yards behind her father. She didn't understand what she was seeing, but it was obvious her father was doing battle with someone, or something.

"Daddy—" she began.

"Shut up," he said benignly, grinning as he unbolted the door for the seventh time. There was a shiver of lunacy in the grin, it was too wide and too easy.

Inexplicably, she returned the smile. It was grim, but genuine. Whatever was at issue here, she loved him.

Polo made a break for the back door. The demon was three paces ahead of him, scooting through the house like a sprinter, and bolting the door before Jack could even reach the handle. The key was turned in the lock by invisible hands, then crushed to dust in the air.

Jack feigned a move towards the window beside the back door but the blinds were pulled down and the shutters slammed. The Yattering, too concerned with the window to watch Jack closely, missed his doubling back through the house.

When it saw the trick that was being played it let out a little screech, and gave chase, almost sliding into Jack on the smoothly polished floor. It avoided the collision only by the most balletic of maneuvers. That would be fatal indeed: to touch the man in the heat of the moment.

Polo was again at the front door and Gina, wise to her

father's strategy, had unbolted it while the Yattering and Jack fought at the back door. Jack had prayed she'd take the opportunity to open it. She had. It stood slightly ajar: the icy air of the crisp afternoon curled its way into the hallway.

Jack covered the last yards to the door in a flash, feeling without hearing the howl of complaint the Yattering loosed as it saw its victim escaping into the outside world.

It was not an ambitious creature. All it wanted at that moment, beyond any other dream, was to take this human's skull between its palms and make a nonsense of it. Crush it to smithereens, and pour the hot thought out onto the snow. To be done with Jack J. Polo, forever and forever.

Was that so much to ask?

Polo had stepped into the squeaky-fresh snow, his slippers and trouser-bottoms buried in chill. By the time the fury reached the step Jack was already three or four yards away, marching up the path towards the gate. Escaping. Escaping.

The Yattering howled again, forgetting its years of training. Every lesson it had learned, every rule of battle engraved on its skull, was submerged by the simple desire to have Polo's life.

It stepped over the threshold and gave chase. It was an unpardonable transgression. Somewhere in Hell, the powers (long may they hold court; long may they shit light on the heads of the damned) felt the sin, and knew the war for Jack Polo's soul was lost.

Jack felt it too. He heard the sound of boiling water, as the demon's footsteps melted to steam the snow on the path. It was coming after him! The thing had broken the first rule of its existence. It was forfeit. He felt the victory in his spine, and his stomach.

The demon overtook him at the gate. Its breath could clearly be seen in the air, though the body it emanated from had not yet become visible.

Jack tried to open the gate, but the Yattering slammed it shut.

"Che sera, sera," said Jack.

The Yattering could bear it no longer. He took Jack's head in his hands, intending to crush the fragile bone to dust.

The touch was its second sin; and it agonized the Yattering beyond endurance. It bayed like a banshee and reeled away from the contact, sliding in the snow and falling on its back.

It knew its mistake. The lessons it had beaten into it came hurtling back. It knew the punishment too, for leaving the house, for touching the man. It was bound to a new lord, enslaved to this idiot-creature standing over it.

Polo had won.

He was laughing, watching the way the outline of the demon formed in the snow on the path. Like a photograph developing on a sheet of paper, the image of the fury came clear. The law was taking its toll. The Yattering could never hide from its master again. There it was, plain to Polo's eyes, in all its charmless glory. Maroon flesh and bright lidless eye, arms flailing, tail thrashing the snow to slush.

"You bastard," it said. Its accent had an Australian lilt.

"You will not speak unless spoken to," said Polo, with quiet, but absolute, authority. "Understood?"

The lidless eye clouded with humility.

"Yes," the Yattering said.

"Yes, Mister Polo."

"Yes, Mister Polo."

Its tail slipped between its legs like that of a whipped dog.

"You may stand."

"Thank you, Mr. Polo."

It stood. Not a pleasant sight, but one Jack rejoiced in nevertheless.

"They'll have you yet," said the Yattering.

"Who will?"

"You know," it said, hesitantly.

"Name them."

"Beelzebub," it answered, proud to name its old master. "The powers. Hell itself."

"I don't think so," Polo mused. "Not with you bound to me as proof of my skills. Aren't I the better of them?"

The eye looked sullen.

"Aren't I?"

"Yes," it conceded bitterly. "Yes. You are the better of them."

It had begun to shiver.

"Are you cold?" asked Polo.

It nodded, affecting the look of a lost child.

"Then you need some exercise," he said. "You'd better go back into the house and start tidying up."

The fury looked bewildered, even disappointed, by this instruction.

"Nothing more?" it asked incredulously. "No miracles? No Helen of Troy? No flying?"

The thought of flying on a snow-spattered afternoon like this left Polo cold. He was essentially a man of simple tastes: all he asked for in life was the love of his children, a pleasant home and a good trading price for gherkins.

"No flying," he said.

As the Yattering slouched down the path towards the door it seemed to alight upon a new piece of mischief. It turned back to Polo, obsequious, but unmistakably smug.

"Could I just say something?" it said.

"Speak."

"It's only fair that I inform you that it's considered ungodly to have any contact with the likes of me. Heretical even."

"Is that so?"

"Oh yes," said the Yattering, warming to its prophecy. "People have been burned for less."

"Not in this day and age," Polo replied.

"But the Seraphim will see," it said. "And that means you'll never go to that place."

"What place?"

The Yattering fumbled for the special word it had heard Beelzebub use.

"Heaven," it said, triumphant. An ugly grin had come on its face; this was the cleverest maneuver it had ever attempted; it was juggling theology here.

Jack nodded slowly, nibbling at his bottom lip.

The creature was probably telling the truth: association with it or its like would not be looked upon benignly by the Host of Saints and Angels. He probably *was* forbidden access to the plains of paradise.

"Well," he said, "you know what I have to say about that, don't you?"

The Yattering stared at him, frowning. No, it didn't know. Then the grin of satisfaction it had been wearing died, as it saw just what Polo was driving at.

"What do I say?" Polo asked it.

Defeated, the Yattering murmured the phrase.

"Che sera, sera."

Polo smiled. "There's a chance for you yet," he said, and led the way over the threshold, closing the door with something very like serenity on his face.

PIG BLOOD BLUES

Y OU COULD SMELL THE KIDS BEFORE YOU could see them, their young sweat turned stale in corridors with barred windows, their bolted breath sour, their heads musty. Then their voices, subdued by the rules of confinement.

Don't run. Don't shout. Don't whistle. Don't fight.

They called it a Remand Center for Adolescent Offenders, but it was near as damn it a prison. There were locks and keys and warders. The gestures of liberalism were few and far between and they didn't disguise the truth too well; Tetherdowne was a prison by a sweeter name, and the inmates knew it.

Not that Redman had any illusions about his pupils-to-be. They were hard, and they were locked away for a reason. Most of them would rob you blind as soon as look at you; cripple you if it suited them, no sweat. He had too many years in the force to believe the sociological lie. He knew the victims, and he knew the kids. They weren't misunderstood morons, they were quick and sharp and amoral, like the razors they hid under their tongues. They had no use for sentiment, they just wanted out.

"Welcome to Tetherdowne."

Was the woman's name Leverton, or Leverfall, or—

"I'm Doctor Leverthal."

Leverthal. Yes. Hard-bitten bitch he'd met at—

"We met at the interview."

"Yes."

"We're glad to see you, Mr. Redman."

"Neil; please call me Neil."

"We try not to go on a first-name basis in front of the boys, we find they think they've got a finger into your private life. So I'd prefer you to keep Christian names purely for off-duty hours."

She didn't offer hers. Probably something flinty. Yvonne. Lydia. He'd invent something appropriate. She looked fifty, and was probably ten years younger. No makeup, hair tied back so severely he wondered her eyes didn't pop.

"You'll be beginning classes the day after tomorrow. The Governor asked me to welcome you to the Center on his behalf, and apologise to you that he can't be here himself. There are funding problems."

"Aren't there always?"

"Regrettably yes. I'm afraid we're swimming against the tide here; the general mood of the country is very Law and Order orientated."

What was that a nice way of saying? Beat the shit out of any kid caught so much as jaywalking? Yes, he'd been that way himself in his time, and it was a nasty little cul-de-sac, every bit as bad as being sentimental.

"The fact is, we may lose Tetherdowne altogether," she said, "which would be a shame. I know it doesn't look like much . . ."

"—but it's home," he laughed. The joke fell among thieves. She didn't even seem to hear it.

"You"—her tone hardened—"you have a solid (did she say sullied?) background in the Police Force. Our hope is that your appointment here will be welcomed by the funding authorities."

So that was it. Token ex-policeman brought in to appease the powers that be, to show willing in the discipline department. They didn't really want him here. They wanted some sociologist who'd write up reports on the effect of the class-system on brutality amongst teenagers. She was quietly telling him that he was the odd man out.

"I told you why I left the force."

"You mentioned it. Invalided out."

"I wouldn't take a desk job, it was as simple as that;

and they wouldn't let me do what I did best. Danger to myself according to some of them."

She seemed a little embarrassed by his explanation. Her a psychologist too; she should have been devouring this stuff, it was his private hurt he was making public here. He was coming clean, for Christ's sake.

"So I was out on my backside, after twenty-four years." He hesitated, then said his piece. "I'm not a token policeman; I'm not any kind of policeman. The force and I parted company. Understand what I'm saying?"

"Good, good." She didn't understand a bloody word. He tried another approach.

"I'd like to know what the boys have been told."

"Been told?"

"About me."

"Well, something of your background."

"I see." They'd been warned. Here come the pigs.

"It seemed important."

He grunted.

"You see, so many of these boys have real aggression problems. That's a source of difficulty for so very many of them. They can't control themselves, and consequently they suffer."

He didn't argue, but she looked at him severely, as though he had.

"Oh yes, they suffer. That's why we're at such pains to show some appreciation of their situation; to teach them that there are alternatives."

She walked across to the window. From the second story there was an adequate view of the grounds. Tetherdowne had been some kind of estate, and there was a good deal of land attached to the main house. A playing field, its grass sere in the midsummer drought. Beyond it a cluster of out-houses, some exhausted trees, shrubbery, and then rough wasteland off to the wall. He'd seen the wall from the other side. Alcatraz would have been proud of it.

"We try to give them a little freedom, a little education and a little sympathy. There's a popular notion, isn't there, that delinquents enjoy their criminal activities? This isn't my experience at all. They come to me guilty, broken . . ."

One broken victim flicked a vee at Leverthal's back as he sauntered along the corridor. Hair slicked down and parted in three places. A couple of home-grown tattoos on his forearm, unfinished.

"They have committed criminal acts, however," Redman pointed out.

"Yes, but—"

"And must, presumably, be reminded of the fact."

"I don't think they need any reminding, Mr. Redman. I think they burn with guilt."

She was hot on guilt, which didn't surprise him. They'd taken over the pulpit, these analysts. They were up where the Bible-thumpers used to stand, with the threadbare sermons on the fires below, but with a slightly less colorful vocabulary. It was fundamentally the same story though, complete with the promises of healing, if the rituals were observed. And behold, the righteous shall inherit the Kingdom of Heaven.

There was a pursuit on the playing field, he noticed. Pursuit, and now a capture. One victim was laying into another, smaller victim with his boot; it was a fairly merciless display.

Leverthal caught the scene at the same time as Redman.

"Excuse me. I must—"

She started down the stairs.

"Your workshop is third door on the left if you want to take a look," she called over her shoulder. "I'll be right back."

Like hell she would. Judging by the way the scene on the field was progressing, it would be a three-crowbar job to prize them apart.

Redman wandered along to his workshop. The door was locked, but through the wired glass he could see the benches, the vises, the tools. Not bad at all. He might even teach them some woodwork, if he was left alone long enough to do it.

A bit frustrated not to be able to get in, he doubled back along the corridor, and followed Leverthal downstairs, finding his way out easily onto the sun-lit playing field. A little knot of spectators had grown around the fight, or the massacre, which had now ceased. Leverthal was standing, staring down at the boy on the ground. One of the warders was kneeling at the boy's head; the injuries looked bad.

A number of the spectators looked up and stared at the new face as Redman approached. There were whispers amongst them, some smiles.

Redman looked at the boy. Perhaps sixteen, he lay with his cheek to the ground, as if listening for something in the earth.

"Lacey," Leverthal named the boy for Redman.

"Is he badly hurt?"

The man kneeling beside Lacey shook his head.

"Not too bad. Bit of a fall. Nothing broken."

There was blood on the boy's face from his mashed nose. His eyes were closed. Peaceful. He could have been dead.

"Where's the bloody stretcher?" said the warder. He was clearly uncomfortable on the drought-hardened ground.

"They're coming, sir," said someone. Redman thought it was the aggressor. A thin lad: about nineteen. The sort of eyes that could sour milk at twenty paces.

Indeed a small posse of boys was emerging from the main building, carrying a stretcher and a red blanket. They were all grinning from ear to ear.

The band of spectators had begun to disperse, now that the best of it was over. Not much fun picking up the pieces.

"Wait, wait," said Redman, "don't we need some witnesses here? Who did this?"

There were a few casual shrugs, but most of them played deaf. They sauntered away as if nothing had been said.

Redman said: "We saw it. From the window."

Leverthal was offering no support.

"Didn't we?" he demanded of her.

"It was too far to lay any blame, I think. But I don't want to see any more of this kind of bullying, do you all understand me?"

She'd seen Lacey, and recognized him easily from that distance. Why not the attacker too? Redman kicked himself for not concentrating; without names and personalities to go with the faces, it was difficult to distinguish between them. The risk of making a misplaced accusation was high, even though he was almost sure of the curdling-eyed boy. This was no time to make mistakes, he decided; this time he'd have to let the issue drop.

Leverthal seemed unmoved by the whole thing.

"Lacey," she said quietly, "it's always Lacey."

"He asks for it," said one of the boys with the stretcher, brushing a sheaf of blond-white hair from his eyes, "he doesn't know no better."

Ignoring the observation, Leverthal supervised Lacey's transfer to the stretcher, and started to walk back to the main building, with Redman in tow. It was all so casual.

"Not exactly wholesome, Lacey," she said cryptically, almost by way of explanation; and that was all. So much for compassion.

Redman glanced back as they tucked the red blanket around Lacey's still form. Two things happened, almost simultaneously.

The first: somebody in the group said, "That's the pig."

The second: Lacey's eyes opened and looked straight into Redman's, wide, clear and true.

⁜

REDMAN SPENT A GOOD DEAL OF THE NEXT DAY putting his workshop in order. Many of the tools had been broken or rendered useless by untrained handling: saws without teeth, chisels that were chipped and edgeless, broken vises. He'd need money to resupply the shop with the basics of the trade, but now wasn't the time to start asking. Wiser to wait, and be seen to do a decent job. He was quite used to the politics of institutions; the force was full of it.

About four-thirty a bell started to ring, a good way from the workshop. He ignored it, but after a time his instincts got the better of him. Bells were alarms, and alarms were sounded to alert people. He left his tidying, locked the workshop door behind him and followed his ears.

The bell was ringing in what was laughingly called the Hospital Unit, two or three rooms closed off from the main block and prettied up with a few pictures and curtains at the windows. There was no sign of smoke in the air, so it clearly wasn't a fire. There was shouting though. More than shouting. A howl.

He quickened his pace along the interminable corridors, and as he turned a corner towards the Unit a small figure ran straight into him. The impact winded both of them, but Redman grabbed the lad by the arm before he could make off again. The captive was quick to respond, lashing out with his shoeless feet against Redman's shin. But he had him fast.

"Let me go, you fucking—"

"Calm down! Calm down!"

His pursuers were almost there.

"Hold him!"

"Fucker! Fucker! Fucker! Fucker!"

"Hold him!"

It was like wrestling a crocodile: the kid had all the strength of fear. But the best of his fury was spent. Tears were springing into his bruised eyes as he spat in Redman's face. It was Lacey in his arms, unwholesome Lacey.

"OK. We got him."

Redman stepped back as the warder took over, putting Lacey in a hold that looked fit to break the boy's arm.

Two or three others were appearing round the corner. Two boys, and a nurse, a very unlovely creature.

"Let me go . . . Let me go . . ." Lacey was yelling, but any stomach for the fight had gone out of him. A pout came to his face in defeat, and still the cow-like eyes turned up accusingly at Redman, big and brown. He looked younger than his sixteen years, almost prepubescent. There was a whisper of bum-fluff on his cheek and a few spots amongst the bruises and a badly applied dressing across his nose. But quite a girlish face, a virgin's face, from an age when there were still virgins. And still the eyes.

Leverthal had appeared, too late to be of use.

"What's going on?"

The warder piped up. The chase had taken his breath, and his temper.

"He locked himself in the lavatories. Tried to get out through the window."

"Why?"

The question was addressed to the warder, not to the child. A telling confusion. The warder, confounded, shrugged.

"Why?" Redman repeated the question to Lacey.

The boy just stared, as though he'd never been asked a question before.

"You the pig?" he said suddenly, snot running from his nose.

"Pig?"

"He means policeman," said one of the boys. The noun was spoken with a mocking precision, as though he was addressing an imbecile.

"I know what he means, lad," said Redman, still determined to out-stare Lacey, "I know very well what he means."

"Are you?"

"Be quiet, Lacey," said Leverthal, "you're in enough trouble as it is."

"Yes, son. I'm the pig."

The war of looks went on, a private battle between boy and man.

"You don't know nothing," said Lacey. It wasn't a snide remark, the boy was simply telling his version of the truth; his gaze didn't flicker.

"All right, Lacey, that's enough." The warder was trying to haul him away; his belly stuck out between pyjama top and bottom, a smooth dome of milk skin.

"Let him speak," said Redman. "What don't I know?"

"He can give his side of the story to the Governor," said Leverthal before Lacey could reply. "It's not your concern."

But it was very much his concern. The stare made it his concern; so cutting, so damned. The stare demanded that it become his concern.

"Let him speak," said Redman, the authority in his voice overriding Leverthal. The warder loosened his hold just a little.

"Why did you try and escape, Lacey?"

"'Cause he came back."

"Who came back? A name, Lacey. Who are you talking about?"

For several seconds Redman sensed the boy fighting a pact with silence; then Lacey shook his head, breaking the electric exchange between them. He seemed to lose his way somewhere; a kind of puzzlement gagged him.

"No harm's going to come to you."

Lacey stared at his feet, frowning. "I want to go back to bed now," he said. A virgin's request.

"No harm, Lacey. I promise."

The promise seemed to have precious little effect; Lacey was struck dumb. But it was a promise nevertheless, and he hoped Lacey realized that. The kid looked exhausted by the effort of his failed escape, of the pursuit, of staring. His face was ashen. He let the warder turn him and take him back. Before he rounded the corner again, he seemed to change his mind; he struggled to loose himself, failed, but managed to twist himself round to face his interrogator.

"Henessey," he said, meeting Redman's eyes once more. That was all. He was shunted out of sight before he could say anything more.

"Henessey?" said Redman, feeling like a stranger suddenly. "Who's Henessey?"

Leverthal was lighting a cigarette. Her hands were shaking ever so slightly as she did it. He hadn't noticed that yesterday, but he wasn't surprised. He'd yet to meet a head shrinker who didn't have problems of their own.

"The boy's lying," she said. "Henessey's no longer with us."

A little pause. Redman didn't prompt, it would only make her jumpy.

"Lacey's clever," she went on, putting the cigarette to her colorless lips. "He knows just the spot."

"Eh?"

"You're new here, and he wants to give you the impression that he's got a mystery all of his own."

"It isn't a mystery then?"

"Henessey?" she snorted. "Good God no. He escaped custody in early May. He and Lacey . . ." She hesitated, without wanting to. "He and Lacey had something between them. Drugs perhaps, we never found out. Glue-sniffing, mutual masturbation, God knows what."

She really did find the whole subject unpleasant. Distaste was written over her face in a dozen tight places.

"How did Henessey escape?"

"We still don't know," she said. "He just didn't turn up for roll-call one morning. The place was searched from top to bottom. But he'd gone."

"Is it possible he'd come back?"

A genuine laugh.

"Jesus no. He hated the place. Besides, how could he get in?"

"He got out."

Leverthal conceded the point with a murmur. "He wasn't especially bright, but he was cunning. I wasn't altogether surprised when he went missing. The few weeks before his escape he'd really sunk into himself. I couldn't get anything out of him, and up until then he'd been quite talkative."

"And Lacey?"

"Under his thumb. It often happens. Younger boy idolizes an older, more experienced individual. Lacey had a very unsettled family background."

Neat, thought Redman. So neat he didn't believe a word of it. Minds weren't pictures at an exhibition, all numbered, and hung in order of influence, one marked "Cunning," the next, "Impressionable." They were scrawls; they were sprawling splashes of graffiti, unpredictable, unconfinable.

And little boy Lacey? He was written on water.

❖

CLASSES BEGAN THE NEXT DAY, IN A HEAT SO oppressive it turned the workshop into an oven by eleven. But the boys responded quickly to Redman's straight dealing. They recognized in him a man they could respect without liking. They expected no favors, and received none. It was a stable agreement.

Redman found the staff on the whole less communicative than the boys. An odd-ball bunch, all in all. Not a strong heart amongst them, he decided. The routine of Tetherdowne, its rituals of classification, of humiliation, seemed to grind them into a common gravel. Increasingly he found himself avoiding conversation with his peers. The workshop became a sanctuary, a home from home, smelling of newly cut wood and bodies.

It was not until the following Monday that one of the boys mentioned the farm.

Nobody had told him there was a farm on the grounds of the Center, and the idea struck Redman as absurd.

"Nobody much goes down there," said Creeley, one of the worst woodworkers on God's earth. "It stinks."

General laughter.

"All right, lads, settle down."

The laughter subsided, laced with a few whispered jibes.

"Where is this farm, Creeley?"

"It's not even a farm really, sir," said Creeley, chewing his tongue (an incessant routine). "It's just a few huts. Stink, they do, sir. Especially now."

He pointed out of the window to the wilderness beyond the playing field. Since he'd last looked out at the sight, that first day with Leverthal, the wasteland had ripened in the sweaty heat, ranker with weeds than ever. Creeley pointed out a distant brick wall, all but hidden behind a shield of shrubs.

"See it, sir?"

"Yes, I see it."

"That's the sty, sir."

Another round of sniggers.

"What's so funny?" He wheeled on the class. A dozen heads snapped down to their work.

"I wouldn't go down there, sir. It's high as a fucking kite."

❖

CREELEY WASN'T EXAGGERATING. EVEN IN THE relative cool of the late afternoon the smell wafting off the farm was stomach turning. Redman just followed his nose across the field and past the out-houses. The buildings he glimpsed from the workshop window were coming out of hiding. A few ramshackle huts thrown up out of corrugated iron and rotting wood, a chicken run, and the brick-built sty were all the farm could offer. As Creeley had said, it wasn't really a farm at all. It was a tiny domesticated Dachau; filthy and forlorn. Somebody obviously fed the few prisoners: the hens, the half dozen geese, the pigs, but nobody seemed bothered to clean them out. Hence that rotten smell. The pigs particularly were living in a bed of their own ordure, islands of dung cooked to perfection in the sun, peopled with thousands of flies.

The sky itself was divided into two separate compartments, divided by a high brick wall. In the forecourt of one a small, mottled pig lay on its side in the filth, its flank alive with ticks and bugs. Another, smaller pig could be glimpsed in the gloom of the interior, lying on shit-thick straw. Neither showed any interest in Redman.

The other compartment seemed empty.

There was no excrement in the forecourt, and far fewer flies amongst the straw. The accumulated smell of old fecal matter was no less acute however and Redman was about to turn away when there was a noise from inside, and a great bulk righted itself. He leaned over the padlocked wooden gate, blotting out the stench by an act of will, and peered through the doorway of the sty.

The pig came out to look at him. It was three times the size of its companions, a vast sow that might well have mothered the pigs in the adjacent pen. But where her farrow were filthy-flanked, the sow was pristine, her blushing pink frame radiant with good health. Her sheer size impressed Redman. She must have weighed twice what he weighed, he guessed: an altogether formidable creature. A glamorous animal in her gross way, with her curling blond lashes and the delicate down on her shiny snout that coarsened to bristles around her lolling ears, and the oily, fetching look in her dark brown eyes.

Redman, a city boy, had seldom seen the living truth behind, or previous to, the meat on his plate. This wonderful porker came as a revelation. The bad press that he'd always believed about pigs, the reputation that made the very name a synonym for foulness, all that was given the lie.

The sow was beautiful, from her snuffling snout to the delicate corkscrew of her tail, a seductress on trotters.

Her eyes regarded Redman as an equal, he had no doubt of that, admiring him rather less than he admired her.

She was safe in her head, he in his. They were equal under a glittering sky.

Close to, her body smelt sweet. Somebody had clearly been there that very morning, sluicing her down, and feeding her. Her trough, Redman now noticed, still brimmed with a mush of slops, the remains of yesterday's meal. She hadn't touched it; she was no glutton.

Soon she seemed to have the sum of him, and grunting quietly she turned around on her nimble feet and returned to the cool of the interior. The audience was over.

⁂

THAT NIGHT HE WENT TO FIND LACEY. THE BOY has been removed from the Hospital Unit and put in a shabby room of his own. He was apparently still being bullied by the other boys in his dormitory, and the alternative was this solitary confinement. Redman found him sitting on a carpet of old comic books, staring at the wall. The lurid covers of the comics made his face look milkier than ever. The bandage had gone from his nose, and the bruise on the bridge was yellowing.

He shook Lacey's hand, and the boy gazed up at him. There was a real turn about since their last meeting. Lacey was calm, even docile. The handshake, a ritual Redman had introduced whenever he met boys out of the workshop, was weak.

"Are you well?"

The boy nodded.

"Do you like being alone?"

"Yes, sir."

"You'll have to go back to the dormitory eventually."

Lacey shook his head.

"You can't stay here forever, you know."

"Oh, I know that, sir."

"You'll have to go back."

Lacey nodded. Somehow the logic didn't seem to have got through to the boy. He turned up the corner of a Superman comic and stared at the splash-page without scanning it.

"Listen to me, Lacey. I want you and I to understand each other. Yes?"

"Yes, sir."

"I can't help you if you lie to me. Can I?"

"No."

PIG BLOOD BLUES

"Why did you mention Kevin Henessey's name to me last week? I know that he isn't here any longer. He escaped, didn't he?"

Lacey stared at the three-color hero on the page.

"Didn't he?"

"He's here," said Lacey, very quietly. The kid was suddenly distraught. It was in his voice, and in the way his face folded up on itself.

"If he escaped, why should he come back? That doesn't really make much sense to me, does it make much sense to you?"

Lacey shook his head. There were tears in his nose, which muffled his words, but they were clear enough.

"He never went away."

"What? You mean he never escaped?"

"He's clever, sir. You don't know Kevin. He's clever."

He closed the comic, and looked up at Redman.

"In what way clever?"

"He planned everything, sir. All of it."

"You have to be clear."

"You won't believe me. Then that's the end, because you won't believe me. He hears, you know, he's everywhere. He doesn't care about walls. Dead people don't care about nothing like that."

Dead. A smaller word than alive; but it took the breath away.

"He can come and go," said Lacey, "anytime he wants."

137

"Are you saying Henessey is dead?" said Redman. "Be careful, Lacey."

The boy hesitated: he was aware that he was walking a tight rope, very close to losing his protector.

"You promised," he said suddenly, cold as ice.

"Promised no harm would come to you. It won't. I said that and I meant it. But that doesn't mean you can tell me lies, Lacey."

"What lies, sir?"

"Henessey isn't dead."

"He is, sir. They all know he is. He hanged himself. With the pigs."

Redman had been lied to many times, by experts, and he felt he'd become a good judge of liars. He knew all the telltale signs. But the boy exhibited none of them. He was telling the truth. Redman felt it in his bones.

The truth; the whole truth; nothing but.

That didn't mean that what the boy was saying was true. He was simply telling the truth as he understood it. He *believed* Henessey was deceased. That proved nothing.

"If Henessey were dead—"

"He *is*, sir."

"If he were, how could he be here?"

The boy looked at Redman without a trace of guile in his face.

"Don't you believe in ghosts, sir?"

So transparent a solution, it flummoxed Redman.

Henessey was dead, yet Henessey was here. Hence, Henessey was a ghost.

"Don't you, sir?"

The boy wasn't asking a rhetorical question. He wanted, no, he demanded, a reasonable answer to his reasonable question.

"No, boy," said Redman. "No, I don't."

Lacey seemed unruffled by this conflict of opinion.

"You'll see," he said simply. "You'll see."

⁂

IN THE STY AT THE PERIMETER OF THE GROUNDS the great, nameless sow was hungry.

She judged the rhythm of the days, and with their progression her desires grew. She knew that the time for stale slops in a trough was past. Other appetites had taken the place of those piggy pleasures.

She had a taste, since the first time, for food with a certain texture, a certain resonance. It wasn't food she would demand all the time, only when the need came on her. Not a great demand: once in a while, to gobble at the hand that fed her.

She stood at the gate of her prison, listless with anticipation, waiting and waiting. She snaffled, she snorted, her impatience becoming a dull anger. In the adjacent pen her castrated sons, sensing her distress, became agitated in their turn. They knew her nature, and it was dangerous. She had, after all, eaten two of their brothers, living, fresh and wet from her own womb.

Then there were noises through the blue veil of twilight, the soft brushing sound of passage through the nettles, accompanied by the murmur of voices.

Two boys were approaching the sty, respect and caution in every step. She made them nervous, and understandably so. The tales of her tricks were legion.

Didn't she speak, when angered, in that possessed voice, bending her fat, porky mouth to talk with a stolen tongue? Wouldn't she stand on her back trotters sometimes, pink and imperial, and demand that the smallest boys be sent into her shadow to suckle her, naked like her farrow? And wouldn't she beat her vicious heels upon the ground, until the food they brought for her was cut into *petit* pieces and delivered into her maw between trembling finger and thumb? All these things she did.

And worse.

Tonight, the boys knew, they had not brought what she wanted. It was not the meat she was due that lay on the plate they carried. Not the sweet, white meat that she had asked for in that other voice of hers, the meat she could, if she desired, take by force. Tonight the meal was simply stale bacon, filched from the kitchens. The nourishment she really craved, the meat that had been pursued and terrified to engorge the muscle, then bruised like a hammered steak for her delectation, that meat was

140

under special protection. It would take a while to coax it to the slaughter.

Meanwhile they hoped she would accept their apologies and their tears, and not devour them in her anger.

One of the boys had shat his pants by the time he reached the sty-wall, and the sow smelt him. Her voice took on a different timbre, enjoying the piquancy of their fear. Instead of the low snort there was a higher, hotter note out of her. It said: I know, I know. Come and be judged. I know, I know.

She watched them through the slats of the gate, her eyes glinting like jewels in the murky night, brighter than the night because living, purer than the night because wanting.

The boys knelt at the gate, their heads bowed in supplication, the plate they both held lightly covered with a piece of stained muslin.

"Well?" she said. The voice was unmistakable in their ears. His voice, out of the mouth of the pig.

The elder boy, a black kid with a cleft palate, spoke quietly to the shining eyes, making the best of his fear:

"It's not what you wanted. We're sorry."

The other boy, uncomfortable in his crowded trousers, murmured his apology too.

"We'll get him for you though. We will, really. We'll bring him to you very soon, as soon as we possibly can."

"Why not tonight?" said the pig.

"He's being protected."

"A new teacher. Mr. Redman."

The sow seemed to know it already. She remembered the confrontation across the wall, the way he'd stared at her as though she was a zoological specimen. So that was her enemy, that old man. She'd have him. Oh yes.

The boys heard her promise of revenge, and seemed content to have the matter taken out of their hands.

"Give her the meat," said the black boy.

The other one stood up, removing the muslin cloth. The bacon smelt bad, but the sow nevertheless made wet noises of enthusiasm. Maybe she had forgiven them.

"Go on, quickly."

The boy took the first strip of bacon between finger and thumb and proffered it. The sow turned her mouth sideways up to it and ate, showing her yellowish teeth. It was gone quickly. The second, the third, fourth, fifth the same.

The sixth and last piece she took with his fingers, snatched with such elegance and speed the boy could only cry out as her teeth champed through the thin digits and swallowed them. He withdrew his hand from over the sty-wall, and gawped at this mutilation. She had done only a little damage, considering. The top of his thumb and half his index finger had gone. The wounds bled quickly, fully, splashing onto his shirt and his shoes. She grunted and snorted and seemed satisfied.

The boy yelped and ran.

"Tomorrow," said the sow to the remaining supplicant. "Not this old pig-meat. It must be white. White and . . . lacy." She thought that was a fine joke.

"Yes," the boy said. "Yes, of course."

"Without fail," she ordered.

"Yes."

"Or I come for him myself. Do you hear me?"

"Yes."

"I come for him myself, wherever he's hiding. I will eat him in his bed if I wish. In his sleep I will eat off his feet, then his legs, then his balls, then his hips—"

"Yes, yes."

"*I want him,*" said the sow, grinding her trotter in the straw. "He's mine."

⁜

"HENESSEY DEAD?" SAID LEVERTHAL, HEAD still down as she wrote one of her interminable reports. "It's another fabrication. One minute the child says he's in the Center, the next he's dead. The boy can't even get his story straight."

It was difficult to argue with the contradictions unless one accepted the idea of ghosts as readily as Lacey. There was no way Redman was going to try and argue that point with the woman. That part was a nonsense. Ghosts were foolishness; just fears made visible. But the possibility of Henessey's suicide made more sense to Redman. He pressed on with his argument.

"So where did Lacey get this story from, about Henessey's death? It's a funny thing to invent."

She deigned to look up, her face drawn up into itself like a snail in its shell.

"Fertile imaginations are par for the course here. If you heard the tales I've got on tape: the exoticism of some of them would blow your head open."

"Have there been suicides here?"

"In my time?" She thought for a moment, pen poised. "Two attempts. Neither, I think, intended to succeed. Cries for help."

"Was Henessey one?"

She allowed herself a little sneer as she shook her head.

"Henessey was unstable in a completely different direction. He thought he was going to live forever. That was his little dream: Henessey the Nietzschean Superman. He had something close to contempt for the common herd. As far as he was concerned, he was a breed apart. As far beyond the rest of us mere mortals as he was beyond that wretched—"

He knew she was going to say pig, but she stopped just short of the word.

"Those wretched animals on the farm," she said, looking back down at her report.

"Henessey spent time at the farm?"

"No more than any other boy," she lied. "None of

them like farm duties, but it's part of the work rota. Mucking out isn't a very pleasant occupation. I can testify to that."

The lie he knew she'd told made Redman keep back Lacey's final detail: that Henessey's death had taken place in the pig-sty. He shrugged, and took an entirely different tack.

"Is Lacey under medication?"

"Some sedatives."

"Are the boys always sedated when they've been in a fight?"

"Only if they try to make escapes. We haven't got enough staff to supervise the likes of Lacey. I don't see why you're so concerned."

"I want him to trust me. I promised him. I don't want him let down."

"Frankly, all this sounds suspiciously like special pleading. The boy's one of many. No unique problems, and no particular hope of redemption."

"Redemption?" It was a strange word.

"Rehabilitation, whatever you choose to call it. Look, Redman, I'll be frank. There's a general feeling that you're not really playing ball here."

"Oh?"

"We all feel, I think this includes the Governor, that you should let us go about our business the way we're used to. Learn the ropes before you start—"

"Interfering."

She nodded. "It's as good a word as any. You're making enemies."

"Thank you for the warning."

"This job's difficult enough without enemies, believe me."

She attempted a conciliatory look, which Redman ignored. Enemies he could live with, liars he couldn't.

⊹

THE GOVERNOR'S ROOM WAS LOCKED, AS IT HAD been for a full week now. Explanations differed as to where he was. Meetings with funding bodies was a favorite reason touted amongst the staff, though the Secretary claimed she didn't exactly know. There were Seminars at the University he was running, somebody said, to bring some research to bear on the problems of Remand Centers. Maybe the Governor was at one of those. If Mr. Redman wanted, he could leave a message, the Governor would get it.

Back in the workshop, Lacey was waiting for him. It was almost seven-fifteen: classes were well over.

"What are you doing here?"

"Waiting, sir."

"What for?"

"You, sir. I wanted to give you a letter, sir. For me mam. Will you get it to her?"

"You can send it through the usual channels, can't you? Give it to the Secretary, she'll forward it. You're allowed two letters a week."

Lacey's face fell.

"They read them, sir: in case you write something you shouldn't. And if you do, they burn them."

"And you've written something you shouldn't?"

He nodded.

"What?"

"About Kevin. I told her all about Kevin, about what happened to him."

"I'm not sure you've got your facts right about Henessey."

The boy shrugged. "It's true, sir," he said quietly, apparently no longer caring if he convinced Redman or not. "It's true. He's there, sir. In her."

"In who? What are you talking about?"

Maybe Lacey was speaking, as Leverthal had suggested, simply out of his fear. There had to be a limit to his patience with the boy, and this was just about it.

A knock on the door, and a spotty individual called Slape was staring at him through the wired glass.

"Come in."

"Urgent telephone call for you, sir. In the Secretary's Office."

Redman hated the telephone. Unsavory machine: it never brought good tidings.

"Urgent. Who from?"

Slape shrugged and picked at his face.

"Stay with Lacey, will you?"

Slape looked unhappy with the prospect.

"Here, sir?" he asked.

"Here."

"Yes, sir."

"I'm relying on you, so don't let me down."

"No, sir."

Redman turned to Lacey. The bruised look was a wound now. Open, as he wept.

"Give me your letter. I'll take it to the Office."

Lacey had thrust the envelope into his pocket. He retrieved it unwillingly, and handed it across to Redman.

"Say thank you."

"Thank you, sir."

❖

THE CORRIDORS WERE EMPTY.

It was television time, and the nightly worship of the box had begun. They would be glued to the black-and-white set that dominated the Recreation Room, sitting through the pap of Cop Shows and Game Shows and Wars from the World Shows with their jaws open and their minds closed. A hypnotized silence would fall on the assembled company until a promise of violence or a hint of sex. Then the room would erupt in whistles, obscenities, and shouts of encouragement, only to subside again into sullen silence during the dialogue, as they waited for another gun, another breast. He could hear gunfire and music, even now, echoing down the corridor.

The Office was open, but the Secretary wasn't there. Gone home presumably. The clock in the Office said eight-nineteen. Redman amended his watch.

The telephone was on the hook. Whoever had called him had tired of waiting, leaving no message. Relieved as he was that the call wasn't urgent enough to keep the caller hanging on, he now felt disappointed not to be speaking to the outside world. Like Crusoe seeing a sail, only to have it sweep by his island.

Ridiculous: this wasn't his prison. He could walk out whenever he liked. He would walk out that very night: and be Crusoe no longer.

He contemplated leaving Lacey's letter on the desk, but thought better of it. He had promised to protect the boy's interests, and that he would do. If necessary, he'd post the letter himself.

Thinking of nothing in particular, he started back towards the workshop. Vague wisps of unease floated in his system, clogging his responses. Sighs sat in his throat, scowls on his face. This damn place, he said aloud, not meaning the walls and the floors, but the trap they represented. He felt he could die here with his good intentions arrayed around him like flowers round a stiff, and nobody would know, or care, or mourn. Idealism was weakness here, compassion an indulgence. Unease was all: unease and—

Silence.

That was what was wrong. Though the television still popped and screamed down the corridor, there was silence accompanying it. No wolf-whistles, no cat-calls.

Redman darted back to the vestibule and down the corridor to the Recreation Room. Smoking was allowed in this section of the building, and the area stank of stale cigarettes. Ahead, the noise of mayhem continued unabated. A woman screamed somebody's name. A man answered and was cut off by a blast of gunfire. Stories, half-told, hung in the air.

He reached the room, and opened the door.

The television spoke to him. "Get down!"

"He's got a gun!"

Another shot.

The woman, blond, big-breasted, took the bullet in her heart, and died on the sidewalk beside the man she'd loved.

The tragedy went unwatched. The Recreation Room was empty, the old armchairs and graffiti-carved stools placed around the television set for an audience who had better entertainment for the evening. Redman wove between the seats and turned the television off. As the silver-blue fluorescence died, and the insistent beat of the music was cut dead, he became aware, in the gloom, in the hush, of somebody at the door.

"Who is it?"

"Slape, sir."

"I told you to stay with Lacey."

"He had to go, sir."

"Go?"

"He ran off, sir. I couldn't stop him."

"Damn you. What do you mean, you couldn't stop him?"

Redman started to re-cross the room, catching his foot on a stool. It scraped on the linoleum, a little protest.

Slape twitched.

"I'm sorry, sir," he said, "I couldn't catch him. I've got a bad foot."

Yes, Slape did limp.

"Which way did he go?"

Slape shrugged.

"Not sure, sir."

"Well, remember."

"No need to lose your temper, sir."

The "sir" was slurred: a parody of respect. Redman found his hand itching to hit this pus-filled adolescent. He was within a couple of feet of the door. Slape didn't move aside.

"Out of my way, Slape."

"Really, sir, there's no way you can help him now. He's gone."

"I said, out of my way."

As he stepped forward to push Slape aside there was a click at navel-level and the bastard had a flick-knife pressed to Redman's belly. The point bit the fat of his stomach.

"There's really no need to go after him, sir."

"What in God's name are you doing, Slape?"

"We're just playing a game," he said through teeth gone grey. "There's no real harm in it. Best leave well alone."

The point of the knife had drawn blood. Warmly, it wended its way down into Redman's groin. Slape was prepared to kill him; no doubt of that. Whatever this game was, Slape was having a little fun all of his own. Killing teacher, it was called. The knife was still being pressed, infinitesimally slowly, through the wall of Redman's flesh. The little rivulet of blood had thickened into a stream.

"Kevin likes to come out and play once in a while," said Slape.

"Henessey?"

"Yes, you like to call us by our second names, don't you? That's more manly, isn't it? That means we're not children, that means we're men. Kevin isn't quite a man though, you see, sir. He's never wanted to be a man. In fact, I think he hated the idea. You know why? (The knife divided muscle now, just gently.) He thought once you were a man, you started to die: and Kevin used to say he'd never die."

"Never die."

"Never."

"I want to meet him."

"Everybody does, sir. He's charismatic. That's the Doctor's word for him: charismatic."

"I want to meet this charismatic fellow."

"Soon."

"Now."

"I said soon."

Redman took the knife-hand at the wrist so quickly Slape had no chance to press the weapon home. The adolescent's response was slow, doped perhaps, and Redman had the better of him. The knife dropped from his hand as Redman's grip tightened, the other hand took Slape in a stranglehold, easily rounding his emaciated neck. Redman's palm pressed on his assailant's Adam's apple, making him gargle.

"Where's Henessey? You take me to him."

The eyes that looked down at Redman were slurred as his words, the irises pin-pricks.

"Take me to him!" Redman demanded.

Slape's hand found Redman's cut belly, and his fist jabbed the wound. Redman cursed, letting his hold slip, and Slape almost slid out of his grasp, but Redman drove his knee into the other's groin, fast and sharp. Slape wanted to double up in agony, but the neck-hold prevented him. The knee rose again, harder. And again. Again.

Spontaneous tears ran down Slape's face, coursing through the minefield of his boils.

"I can hurt you twice as badly as you can hurt me,"

Redman said, "so if you want to go on doing this all night I'm happy as a sandboy."

Slape shook his head, grabbing his breath through his constricted windpipe in short, painful gasps.

"You don't want any more?"

Slape shook his head again. Redman let go of him, and flung him across the corridor against the wall. Whimpering with pain, his face crimped, he slid down the wall into a fetal position, hands between his legs.

"Where's Lacey?"

Slape had begun to shake; the words tumbled out. "Where d'you think? Kevin's got him."

"Where's Kevin?"

Slape looked up at Redman, puzzled.

"Don't you know?"

"I wouldn't ask if I did, would I?"

Slape seemed to pitch forward as he spoke, letting out a sigh of pain. Redman's first thought was that the youth was collapsing, but Slape had other ideas. The knife was suddenly in his hand again, snatched from the floor, and Slape was driving it up towards Redman's groin. He sidestepped the cut with a hair's breadth to spare, and Slape was on his feet again, the pain forgotten. The knife slit the air back and forth, Slape hissing his intention through his teeth.

"Kill you, pig. Kill you, pig."

Then his mouth was wide and he was yelling: "Kevin! Kevin! Help me!"

The slashes were less and less accurate as Slape lost control of himself, tears, snot and sweat sliming his face as he stumbled towards his intended victim.

Redman chose his moment, and delivered a crippling blow to Slape's knee, the weak leg, he guessed. He guessed correctly. Slape screamed, and staggered back, reeling round and hitting the wall face on. Redman followed through, pressing Slape's back. Too late, he realized what he'd done. Slape's body relaxed as his knife hand, crushed between wall and body, slid out, bloody and weaponless. Slape exhaled death-air, and collapsed heavily against the wall, driving the knife still deeper into his own gut. He was dead before he touched the ground.

Redman turned him over. He'd never become used to the suddenness of death. To be gone so quickly, like the image on a television screen. Switched off and blank. No message.

The utter silence of the corridors became overwhelming as he walked back towards the vestibule. The cut on his stomach was not significant, and the blood had made its own scabby bandage of his shirt, knitting cotton to flesh and sealing the wound. It scarcely hurt at all. But the cut was the least of his problems: he had mysteries to unravel now, and he felt unable to face them. The used, exhausted atmosphere of the place made him feel, in his turn, used and exhausted. There was no health to be had here, no goodness, no reason.

He believed, suddenly, in ghosts.

In the vestibule there was a light burning, a bare bulb suspended over the dead space. By it, he read Lacey's crumpled letter. The smudged words on the paper were like matches set to the tinder of his panic.

Mama,

> *They fed me to the pig. Don't believe them if they said I never loved you, or if they said I ran away. I never did. They fed me to the pig. I love you.*

> *Tommy*

He pocketed the letter and began to run out of the building and across the field. It was well dark now: a deep, starless dark, and the air was muggy. Even in daylight he wasn't sure of the route to the farm; it was worse by night. He was very soon lost, somewhere between the playing field and the trees. It was too far to see the outline of the main building behind him, and the trees ahead all looked alike.

The night-air was foul; no wind to freshen tired limbs. It was as still outside as inside, as though the whole world had become an interior: a suffocating room bounded by a painted ceiling of cloud.

He stood in the dark, the blood thumping in his head, and tried to orient himself.

To his left, where he had guessed the out-houses to be, a light glimmered. Clearly he was completely mistaken about his position. The light was at the sty. It threw the ramshackle chicken run into silhouette as he stared at it. There were figures there, several; standing as if watching a spectacle he couldn't yet see.

He started towards the sty, not knowing what he would do once he reached it. If they were all armed like Slape, and shared his murderous intentions, then that would be the end of him. The thought didn't worry him. Somehow tonight to get off of this closed-down world was an attractive option. Down and out.

And there was Lacey. There'd been a moment of doubt, after speaking to Leverthal, when he'd wondered why he cared so much about the boy. That accusation of special pleading, it had a certain truth to it. Was there something in him that wanted Thomas Lacey naked beside him? Wasn't that the subtext of Leverthal's remark? Even now, running uncertainly towards the lights, all he could think of was the boy's eyes, huge and demanding, looking deep into his.

Ahead there were figures in the night, wandering away from the farm. He could see them against the lights of the sty. Was it all over already? He made a long curve around to the left of the buildings to avoid the spectators as they left the scene. They made no noise: there was no chatter or laughter amongst them. Like a congregation leaving a funeral they walked evenly in the dark, each apart from the other, heads bowed. It was eerie, to see these godless delinquents so subdued by reverence.

He reached the chicken run without encountering any of them face-to-face.

There were still a few figures lingering around the pig-house. The wall of the sow's compartment was lined with candles, dozens and dozens of them. They burned steadily in the still air, throwing a rich, warm light onto the brick, and onto the faces of the few who still stared into the mysteries of the sty.

Leverthal was among them, as was the warder who'd knelt at Lacey's head that first day. Two or three boys were there too, whose faces he recognized but could put no name to.

There was a noise from the sty, the sound of the sow's feet on the straw as she accepted their stares. Somebody was speaking, but he couldn't make out who. An adolescent's voice, with a lilt to it. As the voice halted in its monologue, the warder and another of the boys broke rank, as if dismissed, and turned away into the dark. Redman crept a little closer. Time was of the essence now. Soon the first of the congregation would have crossed the field and be back in the Main Building. They'd see Slape's corpse: raise the alarm. He must find Lacey now, if indeed Lacey was still to be found.

Leverthal saw him first. She looked from the sty and nodded a greeting, apparently unconcerned by his arrival.

It was as if his appearance at this place was inevitable, as if all routes led back to the farm, to the straw house and the smell of excrement. It made a kind of sense that she'd believe that. He almost believed it himself.

"Leverthal," he said.

She smiled at him, openly. The boy beside her raised his head and smiled too.

"Are you Henessey?" he asked, looking at the boy.

The youth laughed, and so did Leverthal.

"No," she said. "No. No. No. Henessey is here."

She pointed to the sty.

Redman walked the few remaining yards to the wall of the sty, expecting and not daring to expect the straw and the blood and the pig and Lacey.

But Lacey wasn't there. Just the sow, big and beady as ever, standing amongst pats of her own ordure, her huge, ridiculous ears flapping over her eyes.

"Where's Henessey?" asked Redman, meeting the sow's gaze.

"Here," said the boy.

"This is a pig."

"She ate him," said the youth, still smiling. He obviously thought the idea delightful. "She ate him: and he speaks out of her."

Redman wanted to laugh. This made Lacey's tales of ghosts seem almost plausible by comparison. They were telling him the pig was possessed.

"Did Henessey hang himself, as Tommy said?"

Leverthal nodded.

"In the sty?"

Another nod.

Suddenly the pig took on a different aspect. In his imagination he saw her reaching up to sniff at the feet of Henessey's twitching body, sensing the death coming over it, salivating at the thought of its flesh. He saw her licking the dew that oozed from its skin as it rotted, lapping at it, nibbling daintily at first, then devouring it. It wasn't too difficult to understand how the boys could have made a mythology of that atrocity: inventing hymns to it, attending upon the pig like a god. The candles, the reverence, the intended sacrifice of Lacey: it was evidence of sickness, but it was no more strange than a thousand other customs of faith. He even began to understand Lacey's lassitude, his inability to fight the powers that overtook him.

Mama, they fed me to the pig.

Not Mama, help me, save me. Just: they gave me to the pig.

All this he could understand: they were children, many of them undereducated, some verging on mental instability, all susceptible to superstition. But that didn't explain Leverthal. She was staring into the sty again, and Redman registered for the first time that her hair was unclipped, and lay on her shoulders, honey-colored in the candlelight.

"It looks like a pig to me, plain and simple," he said.

"She speaks with his voice," Leverthal said, quietly.

"Speaks in tongues, you might say. You'll hear him in a while. My darling boy."

Then he understood. "You and Henessey?"

"Don't look so horrified," she said. "He was eighteen: hair blacker than you've ever seen. And he loved me."

"Why did he hang himself?"

"To live forever," she said, "so he'd never be a man and die."

"We didn't find him for six days," said the youth, almost whispering in Redman's ear. "And even then she wouldn't let anybody near him, once she had him to herself. The pig, I mean. Not the Doctor. Everyone loved Kevin, you see," he whispered intimately. "He was beautiful."

"And where's Lacey?"

Leverthal's loving smile decayed.

"With Kevin," said the youth. "Where Kevin wants him."

He pointed through the door of the sty. There was a body lying on the straw, back to the door.

"If you want him, you'll have to go and get him," said the boy, and the next moment he had the back of Redman's neck in a vise-like grip.

The sow responded to the sudden action. She started to stamp the straw, showing the whites of her eyes.

Redman tried to shrug off the boy's grip, at the same time delivering an elbow to his belly. The boy backed off, winded, and cursing, only to be replaced by Leverthal.

"Go to him," she said as she snatched at Redman's

hair. "Go to him if you want him." Her nails raked across his temple and nose, just missing his eyes.

"Get off me!" he said, trying to shake the woman off, but she clung, her head lashing back and forth as she tried to press him over the wall.

The rest happened with horrid speed. Her long hair brushed through a candle flame and her head caught fire, the flames climbing quickly. Shrieking for help she stumbled heavily against the gate. It failed to support her weight, and gave inward. Redman watched helplessly as the burning woman fell amongst the straw. The flames spread enthusiastically across the forecourt towards the sow, lapping up the kindling.

Even now, in extremis, the pig was still a pig. No miracles here: no speaking, or pleading, in tongues. The animal panicked as the blaze surrounded her, cornering her stamping bulk and licking at her flanks. The air was filled with the stench of singeing bacon as the flames ran up her sides and over her head, chasing through her bristles like a grass-fire.

Her voice was a pig's voice, her complaints a pig's complaints. Hysterical grunts escaped her lips and she hurtled across the forecourt of the sty and out of the broken gate, trampling Leverthal.

The sow's body, still burning, was a magic thing in the night as she careered across the field, weaving about in her pain. Her cries did not diminish as the dark ate her up, they seemed just to echo back and forth across the field, unable to find a way out of the locked room.

Redman stepped over Leverthal's fire-ridden corpse and into the sty. The straw was burning on every side, and the fire was creeping towards the door. He half-shut his eyes against the stinging smoke and ducked into the pig-house.

Lacey was lying as he had been all along, back to the door. Redman turned the boy over. He was alive. He was awake. His face, bloated with tears and terror, stared up off his straw pillow, eyes so wide they looked fit to leap from his head.

"Get up," said Redman, leaning over the boy.

His small body was rigid, and it was all Redman could do to prize his limbs apart. With little words of care, he coaxed the boy to his feet as the smoke began to swirl into the pig-house.

"Come on, it's all right, come on."

He stood upright and something brushed his hair. Redman felt a little rain of worms across his face and glanced up to see Henessey, or what was left of him, still suspended from the crossbeam of the pig-house. His features were incomprehensible, blackened to a drooping mush. His body was raggedly gnawed off at the hip, and his innards hung from the fetid carcass, dangling in wormy loops in front of Redman's face.

Had it not been for the thick smoke the smell of the

body would have been overpowering. As it was Redman was simply revolted, and his revulsion gave strength to his arm. He hauled Lacey out of the shadow of the body and pushed him through the door.

Outside the straw was no longer blazing as brightly, but the light of fire and candles and burning body still made him squint after the dark interior.

"Come on, lad," he said, lifting the kid through the flames. The boy's eyes were button-bright, lunatic-bright. They said futility.

They crossed the sty to the gate, skipping Leverthal's corpse, and headed into the darkness of the open field.

The boy seemed to be stirring from his stricken state with every step they took away from the farm. Behind them the sty was already a blazing memory. Ahead, the night was as still and impenetrable as ever.

Redman tried not to think of the pig. It must be dead by now, surely.

But as they ran, there seemed to be a noise in the earth as something huge kept pace with them, content to keep its distance, wary now but relentless in its pursuit.

He dragged on Lacey's arm, and hurried on, the ground sunbaked beneath their feet. Lacey was whimpering now, no words as yet, but sound at least. It was a good sign, a sign Redman needed. He'd had about his fill of insanity.

They reached the building without incident. The corridors were empty as they'd been when he'd left an hour ago. Perhaps nobody had found Slape's corpse yet. It was possible. None of the boys had seemed in a fit mood for recreation. Perhaps they had slipped silently to their dormitories, to sleep off their worship.

It was time to find a phone and call the Police.

Man and boy walked down the corridor towards the Governor's Office hand in hand. Lacey had fallen silent again, but his expression was no longer so manic; it looked as though cleansing tears might be close. He sniffed; made noises in his throat.

His grip on Redman's hand tightened, then relaxed completely.

Ahead, the vestibule was in darkness. Somebody had smashed the bulb recently. It still rocked gently on its cable, illuminated by a seepage of dull light from the window.

"Come on. There's nothing to be afraid of. Come on, boy."

Lacey bent to Redman's hand and bit the flesh. The trick was so quick he let the boy go before he could prevent himself, and Lacey was showing his heels as he scooted away down the corridor away from the vestibule.

No matter. He couldn't get far. For once Redman was glad the place had walls and bars.

Redman crossed the darkened vestibule to the Secretary's Office. Nothing moved. Whoever had broken the bulb was keeping very quiet, very still.

The telephone had been smashed too. Not just broken, smashed to smithereens.

Redman doubled back to the Governor's room. There was a telephone there; he'd not be stopped by vandals.

The door was locked, of course, but Redman was prepared for that. He smashed the frosted glass in the window of the door with his elbow, and reached through to the other side. No key there.

To hell with it, he thought, and put his shoulder to the door. It was sturdy, strong wood, and the lock was good quality. His shoulder ached and the wound in his stomach had reopened by the time the lock gave, and he gained access to the room.

The floor was littered with straw; the smell inside made the sty seem sweet. The Governor was lying behind his desk, his heart eaten out.

"The pig," said Redman. "The pig. The pig." And saying, "the pig," he reached for the phone.

A sound. He turned, and met the blow full-face. It broke his cheek-bone and his nose. The room mottled, and went white.

❖

THE VESTIBULE WAS NO LONGER DARK. CANDLES were burning, it seemed hundreds of them, in every corner, on every edge. But then his head was swimming, his eyesight blurred with concussion. It could have been a single candle, multiplied by senses that could no longer be trusted to tell the truth.

He stood in the middle of the arena of the vestibule, not quite knowing how he could be standing, for his legs felt numb and useless beneath him. At the periphery of his vision, beyond the light of the candles, he could hear people talking. No, not really talking. They weren't proper words. They were nonsense sounds, made by people who may or may not have been there.

Then he heard the grunt, the low, asthmatic grunt of the sow, and straight ahead she emerged from the swimming light of the candles. She was bright and beautiful no longer. Her flanks were charred, her beady eyes withered, her snout somehow twisted out of true. She hobbled towards him very slowly, and very slowly the figure astride her became apparent. It was Tommy Lacey of course, naked as the day he was born, his body as pink and as hairless as one of her farrow, his face as innocent of human feeling. His eyes were now her eyes, as he guided the great sow by her ears. And the noise of the sow, the snaffling sound, was not out of the pig's mouth, but out of his. His was the voice of the pig.

Redman said his name, quietly. Not Lacey, but Tommy. The boy seemed not to hear. Only then, as the pig and her rider approached, did Redman register why he hadn't fallen on his face. There was a rope around his neck.

Even as he thought the thought, the noose tightened, and he was hauled off his feet into the air.

No pain, but a terrible horror, worse, so much worse,

than pain, opened in him, a gorge of loss and regret, and all he was sank away into it.

Below him, the sow and the boy had come to a halt, beneath his jangling feet. The boy, still grunting, had climbed off the pig and was squatting down beside the beast. Through the greying air Redman could see the curve of the boy's spine, the flawless skin of his back. He saw too the knotted rope that protruded from between his pale buttocks, the end frayed. For all the world like the tail of a pig.

The sow put its head up, though its eyes were beyond seeing. He liked to think that she suffered, and would suffer now until she died. It was almost sufficient, to think of that. Then the sow's mouth opened, and she spoke. He wasn't certain how the words came, but they came. A boy's voice, lilting.

"This is the state of the beast," it said, "to eat and be eaten."

Then the sow smiled, and Redman felt, though he had believed himself numb, the first shock of pain as Lacey's teeth bit off a piece from his foot, and the boy clambered, snorting, up his saviour's body to kiss out his life.

SEX, DEATH

AND STARSHINE

＊

DIANE RAN HER SCENTED FINGERS THROUGH the two days' growth of ginger stubble on Terry's chin.

"I love it," she said. "Even the grey bits."

She loved everything about him, or at least that's what she claimed.

When he kissed her: I love it.

When he undressed her: I love it.

When he slid his briefs off: I love it, I love it, I love it.

She'd go down on him with such unalloyed enthusiasm, all he could do was watch the top of her ash-blond head bobbing at his groin, and hope to God nobody chanced to walk into the dressing room. She was a married woman, after all, even if she was an actress. He had a wife himself, somewhere. This tête-à-tête would make some juicy copy for one of the local rags, and here he was trying to garner a reputation as a serious-minded director; no gimmicks, no gossip; just art.

Then, even thoughts of ambition would be dissolved on her tongue, as she played havoc with his nerve-endings. She wasn't much of an actress, but by God she was quite a performer. Faultless technique; immaculate timing: she knew either by instinct or by rehearsal just when to pick up the rhythm and bring the whole scene to a satisfying conclusion.

When she'd finished milking the moment dry, he almost wanted to applaud.

❧

THE WHOLE CAST OF CALLOWAY'S PRODUCTION OF *Twelfth Night* knew about the affair, of course. There'd be the occasional snide comment passed if actress and director were both late for rehearsal, or if she arrived looking full, and he flushed. He tried to persuade her to control the cat-with-the-cream look that crept over her face, but she just wasn't that good a deceiver. Which was rich, considering her profession.

But then La Duvall, as Edward insisted on calling her, didn't need to be a great player, she was famous. So what if she spoke Shakespeare like it was Hiawatha, dum de dum de dum de dum? So what if her grasp of psychology was dubious, her logic faulty, her projection inadequate? So what if she had as much sense of poetry as she did propriety? She was a star, and that meant business.

There was no taking that away from her: her name was money. The Elysium Theater publicity announced her claim to fame in three-inch Roman Bold, black on yellow.

"Diane Duvall: star of *The Love Child*."

The Love Child. Possibly the worst soap opera to cavort across the screens of the nation in the history of that genre, two solid hours a week of under-written characters and mind-numbing dialogue, as a result of which it consistently drew high ratings, and its performers became, almost overnight, brilliant stars in television's rhinestone heaven. Glittering there, the brightest of the bright, was Diane Duvall.

Maybe she wasn't born to play the classics, but Jesus was she good box-office. And in this day and age, with theaters deserted, all that mattered was the number of punters in seats.

Calloway had resigned himself to the fact that this would not be the definitive *Twelfth Night*, but if the production were successful, and with Diane in the role of Viola it had every chance, it might open a few doors to him in the West End. Besides, working with the ever-adoring, ever-demanding Miss D. Duvall had its compensations.

✥

CALLOWAY PULLED UP HIS SERGE TROUSERS, AND looked down at her. She was giving him that winsome smile of hers, the one she used in the letter scene. Expression Five in the Duvall repertoire, somewhere between Virginal and Motherly.

He acknowledged the smile with one from his own stock, a small, loving look that passed for genuine at a yard's distance. Then he consulted his watch.

"God, we're late, sweetie."

She licked her lips. Did she really like the taste that much?

"I'd better fix my hair," she said, standing up and glancing in the long mirror beside the shower.

"Yes."

"Are you OK?"

"Couldn't be better," he replied. He kissed her lightly on the nose and left her to her teasing.

On his way to the stage he ducked into the Men's Dressing Room to adjust his clothing, and dowse his burning cheeks with cold water. Sex always induced a giveaway mottling on his face and upper chest. Bending to splash water on himself Calloway studied his features critically in the mirror over the sink. After thirty-six years of holding the signs of age at bay, he was beginning to look the part. He was no more the juvenile lead. There was an indisputable puffiness beneath his eyes, which was nothing to do with sleeplessness, and there were lines too, on his forehead, and round his mouth. He didn't look the *wunderkind* any longer; the secrets of his debauchery were written all over his face. The excess of sex, booze and ambition, the frustration of aspiring and just missing the main chance so many times. What would he look like now, he thought bitterly, if he'd been content to be some unenterprising nobody working in a minor rep, guaranteed a house of ten aficionados every night, and devoted to Brecht? Face as smooth as a baby's bottom probably, most of the people in the socially committed theater had that look. Vacant and content, poor cows.

Well, you pays your money and you takes your choice, he told himself. He took one last look at the haggard cherub in the mirror, reflecting that, crow's-feet or not, women still couldn't resist him, and went out to face the trials and tribulations of Act III.

On stage there was a heated debate in progress. The carpenter, his name was Jake, had built two hedges for Olivia's garden. They still had to be covered with leaves, but they looked quite impressive, running the depth of the stage to the cyclorama, where the rest of the garden would be painted. None of this symbolic stuff. A garden was a garden: green grass, blue sky. That's the way the audience liked it north of Birmingham, and Terry had some sympathy for their plain tastes.

"Terry, love."

Eddie Cunningham had him by the hand and elbow, escorting him into the fray.

"What's the problem?"

"Terry, love, you cannot be serious about these fucking (it came trippingly off the tongue: fucking) hedges. Tell Uncle Eddie you're not serious before I throw a fit." Eddie pointed towards the offending hedges. "I mean look at them." As he spoke a thin plume of spittle fizzed in the air.

"What's the problem?" Terry asked again.

"Problem? Blocking, love, blocking. *Think* about it. We've rehearsed this whole scene with me bobbing up and down like a March hare. Up right, down left—but it doesn't work if I haven't got access round the back. And look! These fucking things are flush with the backdrop."

"Well, they have to be, for the illusion, Eddie."

"I can't get round though, Terry. You must see my point."

He appealed to the few others on stage: the carpenters, two technicians, three actors.

"I mean—there's just not enough time."

"Eddie, we'll re-block."

"Oh."

That took the wind out of his sails.

"No?"

"Um."

"I mean it seems easiest, doesn't it?"

"Yes . . . I just liked . . ."

"I know."

"Well. Needs must. What about the croquet?"

"We'll cut that too."

"All that business with the croquet mallets? The bawdy stuff?"

"It'll all have to go. I'm sorry, I haven't thought this through. I wasn't thinking straight."

Eddie flounced.

"That's all you ever do, love, think straight . . ."

Titters. Terry let it pass. Eddie had a genuine point of criticism; he had failed to consider the problems of the hedge design.

"I'm sorry about the business; but there's no way we can accommodate it."

"You won't be cutting anybody else's business, I'm sure," said Eddie. He threw a glance over Calloway's shoulder at Diane, then headed for the dressing room. Exit enraged actor, stage left. Calloway made no attempt to stop him. It would have worsened the situation considerably to spoil his departure. He just breathed out a quiet "oh Jesus," and dragged a wide hand down over his face. That was the fatal flaw of this profession: actors.

"Will somebody fetch him back?" he said.

Silence.

"Where's Ryan?"

The Stage Manager showed his bespectacled face over the offending hedge.

"Sorry?"

"Ryan, love—will you please take a cup of coffee to Eddie and coax him back into the bosom of the family?"

Ryan pulled a face that said: You offended him, you fetch him. But Calloway had passed this particular buck before: he was a past master at it. He just stared at Ryan, defying him to contradict his request, until the other man dropped his eyes and nodded his acquiescence.

"Sure," he said glumly.

"Good man."

Ryan cast him an accusatory look, and disappeared in pursuit of Ed Cunningham.

"No show without Belch," said Calloway, trying to warm up the atmosphere a little. Someone grunted: and the small half-circle of onlookers began to disperse. Show over.

"OK, OK," said Calloway, picking up the pieces, "let's get to work. We'll run through from the top of the scene. Diane, are you ready?"

"Yes."

"OK. Shall we run it?"

He turned away from Olivia's garden and the waiting actors just to gather his thoughts. Only the stage working lights were on, the auditorium was in darkness. It yawned at him insolently, row upon row of empty seats, defying him to entertain them. Ah, the loneliness of the long-distance director. There were days in this business when the thought of life as an accountant seemed a consummation devoutedly to be wished, to paraphrase the Prince of Denmark.

In the Gods of the Elysium, somebody moved. Calloway looked up from his doubts and stared through the swarthy air. Had Eddie taken residence in the very back row? No, surely not. For one thing, he hadn't had time to get all the way up there.

"Eddie?" Calloway ventured, capping his hand over his eyes. "Is that you?"

He could just make the figure out. No, not a figure, figures. Two people, edging their way along the back row, making for the exit. Whoever it was, it certainly wasn't Eddie.

"That isn't Eddie, is it?" said Calloway, turning back into the fake garden.

"No," someone replied.

It was Eddie speaking. He was back on stage, leaning on one of the hedges, cigarette clamped between his lips.

"Eddie . . ."

"It's all right," said the actor good-humoredly, "don't grovel. I can't bear to see a pretty man grovel."

"We'll see if we can slot the mallet business in somewhere," said Calloway, eager to be conciliatory.

Eddie shook his head, and flicked ash off his cigarette.

"No need."

"Really—"

"It didn't work too well anyhow."

The Grand Circle door creaked a little as it closed behind the visitors. Calloway didn't bother to look around. They'd gone, whoever they were.

✛

"THERE WAS SOMEBODY IN THE HOUSE THIS afternoon."

Hammersmith looked up from the sheets of figures he was poring over.

"Oh?" His eyebrows were eruptions of wire-thick hair that seemed ambitious beyond their calling. They were raised high above Hammersmith's tiny eyes in patently fake surprise. He plucked at his bottom lip with nicotine-stained fingers.

"Any idea who it was?"

He plucked on, still staring up at the younger man; undisguised contempt on his face.

"Is it a problem?"

"I just want to know who was in looking at the rehearsal, that's all. I think I've got a perfect right to ask."

"Perfect right," said Hammersmith, nodding slightly and making his lips into a pale bow.

"There was talk of somebody coming up from the National," said Calloway. "My agents were arranging something. I just don't want somebody coming in without me knowing about it. Especially if they're important."

Hammersmith was already studying the figures again. His voice was tired.

"Terry: if there's someone in from the South Bank to

look your opus over, I promise you, you'll be the first to be informed. All right?"

The inflexion was so bloody rude. So run-along-little-boy. Calloway itched to hit him.

"I don't want people watching rehearsals unless I authorize it, Hammersmith. Hear me? And I want to know who was in today."

The Manager sighed heavily.

"Believe me, Terry," he said, "I don't know myself. I suggest you ask Tallulah—she was front of house this afternoon. If somebody came in, presumably she saw them."

He sighed again.

"All right . . . Terry?"

Calloway left it at that. He had his suspicions about Hammersmith. The man couldn't give a shit about theater, he never failed to make that absolutely plain; he affected an exhausted tone whenever anything but money was mentioned, as though matters of aesthetics were beneath his notice. And he had a word, loudly administered, for actors and directors alike: butterflies. One-day wonders. In Hammersmith's world only money was forever, and the Elysium Theater stood on prime land, land a wise man could turn a tidy profit on if he played his cards right.

Calloway was certain he'd sell off the place tomorrow if he could maneuver it. A satellite town like Redditch, growing as Birmingham grew, didn't need theaters, it needed offices, hypermarkets, warehouses: it needed, to quote the councillors, growth through investment in new industry. It also needed prime sites to build that industry upon. No mere art could survive such pragmatism.

⚜

TALLULAH WAS NOT IN THE BOX, NOR IN THE foyer, nor in the Green Room.

Irritated both by Hammersmith's incivility and Tallulah's disappearance, Calloway went back into the auditorium to pick up his jacket and go to get drunk. The rehearsal was over and the actors long gone. The bare hedges looked somewhat small from the back row of the stalls. Maybe they needed an extra few inches. He made a note on the back of a show bill he found in his pocket: Hedges, bigger?

A footfall made him look up, and a figure had appeared on stage. A smooth entrance, up-stage center, where the hedges converged. Calloway didn't recognize the man.

"Mr. Calloway? Mr. Terence Calloway?"

"Yes?"

The visitor walked down stage to where, in an earlier age, the footlights would have been, and stood looking out into the auditorium.

"My apologies for interrupting your train of thought."

"No problem."

"I wanted a word."

"With me?"

"If you would."

Calloway wandered down to the front of the stalls, appraising the stranger.

He was dressed in shades of grey from head to foot. A grey worsted suit, grey shoes, a grey cravat. Piss-elegant, was Calloway's first, uncharitable summation. But the man cut an impressive figure nevertheless. His face beneath the shadow of his brim was difficult to discern.

"Allow me to introduce myself."

The voice was persuasive, cultured. Ideal for advertisement voice-overs: soap commercials, maybe. After Hammersmith's bad manners, the voice came as a breath of good breeding.

"My name is Lichfield. Not that I expect that means much to a man of your tender years."

Tender years: well, well. Maybe there was still something of the *wunderkind* in his face.

"Are you a critic?" Calloway inquired.

The laugh that emanated from beneath the immaculately swept brim was ripely ironical.

"In the name of Jesus, no," Lichfield replied.

"I'm sorry, then, you have me at a loss."

"No need for an apology."

"Were you in the house this afternoon?"

Lichfield ignored the question. "I realize you're a busy man, Mr. Calloway, and I don't want to waste your time. The theater is my business, as it is yours. I think we must consider ourselves allies, though we have never met."

Ah, the great brotherhood. It made Calloway want to spit, the familiar claims of sentiment. When he thought of the number of so-called allies that had cheerfully stabbed him in the back; and in return the playwrights whose work he'd smilingly slanged, the actors he'd crushed with a casual quip. Brotherhood be damned, it was dog eat dog, same as any over-subscribed profession.

"I have," Lichfield was saying, "an abiding interest in the Elysium." There was a curious emphasis on the word "abiding." It sounded positively funereal from Lichfield's lips. Abide with me.

"Oh?"

"Yes, I've spent many happy hours in this theater, down the years, and frankly it pains me to carry this burden of news."

"What news?"

"Mr. Calloway, I have to inform you that your *Twelfth Night* will be the last production the Elysium will see."

The statement didn't come as much of a surprise, but it still hurt, and the internal wince must have registered on Calloway's face.

"Ah . . . so you didn't know. I thought not. They always keep the artists in ignorance, don't they? It's a satisfaction the Apollonians will never relinquish. The accountant's revenge."

"Hammersmith," said Calloway.

"Hammersmith."

"Bastard."

"His clan are never to be trusted, but then I hardly need to tell you that."

"Are you sure about the closure?"

"Certainly. He'd do it tomorrow if he could."

"But why? I've done Stoppard here, Tennessee Williams—always played to good houses. It doesn't make sense."

"It makes admirable financial sense, I'm afraid, and if you think in figures, as Hammersmith does, there's no riposte to simple arithmetic. The Elysium's getting old. We're *all* getting old. We creak. We feel our age in our joints: our instinct is to lie down and be gone away."

Gone away: the voice became melodramatically thin, a whisper of longing.

"How do you know about this?"

"I was, for many years, a trustee of the theater and since my retirement I've made it my business to—what's the phrase?—keep my ear to the ground. It's difficult, in this day and age, to evoke the triumph this stage has seen . . ."

His voice trailed away, in a reverie. It seemed true, not an effect.

Then, business-like once more: "This theater is about to die, Mr. Calloway. You will be present at the last rites, through no fault of your own. I felt you ought to be . . . warned."

"Thank you. I appreciate that. Tell me, were you ever an actor yourself?"

"What makes you think that?"

"The voice."

"Too rhetorical by half, I know. My curse, I'm afraid. I can scarcely ask for a cup of coffee without sounding like Lear in the storm."

He laughed heartily, at his own expense. Calloway began to warm to the fellow. Maybe he was a little archaic-looking, perhaps even slightly absurd, but there was a full-bloodedness about his manner that caught Calloway's imagination. Lichfield wasn't apologetic about his love of theater, like so many in the profession, people who trod the boards as a second-best, their souls sold to the movies.

"I have, I will confess, dabbled in the craft a little," Lichfield confided, "but I just don't have the stamina for it, I'm afraid. Now my wife—"

Wife? Calloway was surprised Lichfield had a heterosexual bone in his body.

"—My wife, Constantia, has played here on a number of occasions, and I may say very successfully. Before the war, of course."

"It's a pity to close the place."

"Indeed. But there are no last-act miracles to be performed, I'm afraid. The Elysium will be rubble in six weeks' time, and there's an end to it. I just wanted you to know that interests other than the crassly commercial are watching over this closing production. Think of us as guardian angels. We wish you well, Terence, we all wish you well."

It was a genuine sentiment, simply stated. Calloway was touched by this man's concern, and a little chastened by it. It put his own stepping-stone ambitions in an unflattering perspective. Lichfield went on: "We care to see this theater end its days in suitable style, then die a good death."

"Damn shame."

"Too late for regrets by a long chalk. We should never have given up Dionysus for Apollo."

"What?"

"Sold ourselves to the accountants, to legitimacy, to the likes of Mr. Hammersmith, whose soul, if he has one, must be the size of my fingernail, and grey as a louse's back. We should have had the courage of our depictions, I think. Served poetry and lived under the stars."

Calloway didn't quite follow the allusions, but he got the general drift, and respected the viewpoint.

Off stage left, Diane's voice cut the solemn atmosphere like a plastic knife.

"Terry? Are you there?"

The spell was broken: Calloway hadn't been aware how hypnotic Lichfield's presence was until that other voice came between them. Listening to him was like

being rocked in familiar arms. Lichfield stepped to the
edge of the stage, lowering his voice to a conspiratorial
rasp.

"One last thing, Terence—"

"Yes?"

"Your Viola. She lacks, if you'll forgive my pointing it
out, the special qualities required for the role."

Calloway hung fire.

"I know," Lichfield continued, "personal loyalties
prevent honesty in these matters."

"No," Calloway replied, "you're right. But she's
popular."

"So was bear-baiting, Terence."

A luminous smile spread beneath the brim, hanging
in the shadow like the grin of the Cheshire cat.

"I'm only joking," said Lichfield, his rasp a chuckle
now. "Bears can be charming."

"Terry, there you are."

Diane appeared, over-dressed as usual, from behind
the tabs. There was surely an embarrassing confrontation
in the air. But Lichfield was walking away down the false
perspective of the hedges towards the backdrop.

"Here I am," said Terry.

"Who are you talking to?"

But Lichfield had exited, as smoothly and as quietly as
he had entered. Diane hadn't even seen him go.

"Oh, just an angel," said Calloway.

✢

THE FIRST DRESS REHEARSAL WASN'T, ALL things considered, as bad as Calloway had anticipated: it was immeasurably worse. Cues were lost, props mislaid, entrances missed; the comic business seemed ill-contrived and laborious; the performances either hopelessly overwrought or trifling. This was a *Twelfth Night* that seemed to last a year. Halfway through the third act Calloway glanced at his watch, and realized an uncut performance of *Macbeth* (with interval) would now be over.

He sat in the stalls with his head buried in his hands, contemplating the work that he still had to do if he was to bring this production up to scratch. Not for the first time on this show he felt helpless in the face of the casting problems. Cues could be tightened, props rehearsed with, entrances practiced until they were engraved on the memory. But a bad actor is a bad actor is a bad actor. He could labor 'til doomsday neatening and sharpening, but he could not make a silk purse of the sow's ear that was Diane Duvall.

With all the skill of an acrobat she contrived to skirt every significance, to ignore every opportunity to move the audience, to avoid every nuance the playwright would insist on putting in her way. It was a performance heroic in its ineptitude, reducing the delicate characterization Calloway had been at pains to create to a single-note

189

whine. This Viola was soap-opera pap, less human than the hedges, and about as green.

The critics would slaughter her.

Worse than that, Lichfield would be disappointed. To his considerable surprise the impact of Lichfield's appearance hadn't dwindled; Calloway couldn't forget his actorly projection, his posing, his rhetoric. It had moved him more deeply than he was prepared to admit, and the thought of this *Twelfth Night*, with this Viola, becoming the swan-song of Lichfield's beloved Elysium perturbed and embarrassed him. It seemed somehow ungrateful.

He'd been warned often enough about a director's burdens, long before he became seriously embroiled in the profession. His dear departed guru at the Actor's Center, Wellbeloved (he of the glass eye), had told Calloway from the beginning:

"A director is the loneliest creature on God's earth. He knows what's good and bad in a show, or he should if he's worth his salt, and he has to carry that information around with him and keep smiling."

It hadn't seemed so difficult at the time.

"This job isn't about succeeding," Wellbeloved used to say, "it's about learning not to fall on your sodding face."

Good advice as it turned out. He could still see Wellbeloved handing out that wisdom on a plate, his bald head shiny, his living eye glittering with cynical delight. No man on earth, Calloway had thought, loved theater with more passion than Wellbeloved, and surely no man could have been more scathing about its pretensions.

❖

IT WAS ALMOST ONE IN THE MORNING BY THE time they'd finished the wretched run-through, gone through the notes and separated, glum and mutually resentful, into the night. Calloway wanted none of their company tonight: no late drinking in one or other's digs, no mutual ego-massage. He had a cloud of gloom all to himself, and neither wine, women nor song would disperse it. He could barely bring himself to look Diane in the face. His notes to her, broadcast in front of the rest of the cast, had been acidic. Not that it would do much good.

In the foyer, he met Tallulah, still spry though it was long after an old lady's bedtime.

"Are you locking up tonight?" he asked her, more for something to say than because he was actually curious.

"I always lock up," she said. She was well over seventy: too old for her job in the box office, and too tenacious to be easily removed. But then that was all academic now, wasn't it? He wondered what her response would be when she heard the news of the closure. It would probably break her brittle heart. Hadn't Hammersmith once told him Tallulah had been at the theater since she was a girl of fifteen?

"Well, goodnight, Tallulah."

She gave him a tiny nod, as always. Then she reached out and took Calloway's arm.

"Yes?"

"Mr. Lichfield . . ." she began.

"What about Mr. Lichfield?"

"He didn't like the rehearsal."

"He was in tonight?"

"Oh yes," she replied, as though Calloway was an imbecile for thinking otherwise, "of course he was in."

"I didn't see him."

"Well . . . no matter. He wasn't very pleased."

Calloway tried to sound indifferent.

"It can't be helped."

"Your show is very close to his heart."

"I realize that," said Calloway, avoiding Tallulah's accusing looks. He had quite enough to keep him awake tonight, without her disappointed tones ringing in his ears.

He loosed his arm, and made for the door. Tallulah made no attempt to stop him. She just said: "You should have seen Constantia."

Constantia? Where had he heard that name? Of course, Lichfield's wife.

"She was a wonderful Viola."

He was too tired for this mooning over dead actresses;

she was dead, wasn't she? He had said she was dead, hadn't he?

"Wonderful," said Tallulah again.

"Goodnight, Tallulah. I'll see you tomorrow."

The old crone didn't answer. If she was offended by his brusque manner, then so be it. He left her to her complaints and faced the street.

It was late November, and chilly. No balm in the night air, just the smell of tar from a freshly laid road, and grit in the wind. Calloway pulled his jacket collar up around the back of his neck, and hurried off to the questionable refuge of Murphy's Bed and Breakfast.

In the foyer Tallulah turned her back on the cold and dark of the outside world, and shuffled back into the temple of dreams. It smelt so weary now: stale with use and age, like her own body. It was time to let natural processes take their toll; there was no point in letting things run beyond their allotted span. That was as true of buildings as of people. But the Elysium had to die as it had lived, in glory.

Respectfully, she drew back the red curtains that covered the portraits in the corridor that led from foyer to stalls. Barrymore, Irving: great names and great actors. Stained and faded pictures perhaps, but the memories were as sharp and as refreshing as spring water. And in pride of place, the last of the line to be unveiled, a portrait of Constantia Lichfield. A face of transcendent beauty; a bone structure to make an anatomist weep.

She had been far too young for Lichfield of course, and that had been part of the tragedy of it. Lichfield the Svengali, a man twice her age, had been capable of giving his brilliant beauty everything she desired: fame, money, companionship. Everything but the gift she most required: life itself.

She'd died before she was yet twenty, a cancer in the breast. Taken so suddenly it was still difficult to believe she'd gone.

Tears brimmed in Tallulah's eyes as she remembered that lost and wasted genius. So many parts Constantia would have illuminated had she been spared. Cleopatra, Hedda, Rosalind, Electra . . .

But it wasn't to be. She'd gone, extinguished like a candle in a hurricane, and for those who were left behind life was a slow and joyless march through a cold land. There were mornings now, stirring to another dawn, when she would turn over and pray to die in her sleep.

The tears were quite blinding her now, she was awash. And oh dear, there was somebody behind her, probably Mr. Calloway back for something, and here she was, sobbing fit to burst, behaving like the silly old woman she knew he thought her to be. A young man like him, what did he understand about the pain of the years, the deep ache of irretrievable loss? That wouldn't come to him for a while yet. Sooner than he thought, but a while nevertheless.

"Tallie," somebody said.

She knew who it was. Richard Walden Lichfield. She

turned round and he was standing no more than six feet from her, as fine a figure of a man as ever she remembered him to be. He must be twenty years older than she was, but age didn't seem to bow him. She felt ashamed of her tears.

"Tallie," he said kindly, "I know it's a little late, but I felt you'd surely want to say hello."

"Hello?"

The tears were clearing, and now she saw Lichfield's companion, standing a respectful foot or two behind him, partially obscured. The figure stepped out of Lichfield's shadow and there was a luminous, fine-boned beauty Tallulah recognized as easily as her own reflection. Time broke in pieces, and reason deserted the world. Longed-for faces were suddenly back to fill the empty nights, and offer fresh hope to a life grown weary. Why should she argue with the evidence of her eyes?

It was Constantia, the radiant Constantia, who was looping her arm through Lichfield's and nodding gravely at Tallulah in greeting.

Dear, dead Constantia.

❖

THE REHEARSAL WAS CALLED FOR NINE-THIRTY the following morning. Diane Duvall made an entrance her customary half hour late. She looked as though she hadn't slept all night.

"Sorry I'm late," she said, her open vowels oozing down the aisle towards the stage.

Calloway was in no mood for foot-kissing.

"We've got an opening tomorrow," he snapped, "and everybody's been kept waiting by you."

"Oh really?" she fluttered, trying to be devastating. It was too early in the morning, and the effect fell on stony ground.

"OK, we're going from the top," Calloway announced, "and everybody please have your copies and a pen. I've got a list of cuts here and I want them rehearsed in by lunchtime. Ryan, have you got the prompt copy?"

There was a hurried exchange with the ASM and an apologetic negative from Ryan.

"Well, get it. And I don't want any complaints from anyone, it's too late in the day. Last night's run was a wake, not a performance. The cues took forever; the business was ragged. I'm going to cut, and it's not going to be very palatable."

It wasn't. The complaints came, warning or no, the arguments, the compromises, the sour faces and muttered insults. Calloway would have rather been hanging by his toes from a trapeze than maneuvering fourteen highly strung people through a play two-thirds of them scarcely understood, and the other third couldn't give a monkey's about. It was nerve-wracking.

It was made worse because all the time he had the prickly sense of being watched, though the auditorium was empty from Gods to front stalls. Maybe Lichfield had a spyhole somewhere, he thought, then condemned the idea as the first sign of budding paranoia.

At last, lunch.

Calloway knew where he'd find Diane, and he was prepared for the scene he had to play with her. Accusations, tears, reassurance, tears again, reconciliation. Standard format.

He knocked on the Star's door.

"Who is it?"

Was she crying already, or talking through a glass of something comforting?

"It's me."

"Oh."

"Can I come in?"

"Yes."

She had a bottle of vodka, good vodka, and a glass. No tears as yet.

"I'm useless, aren't I?" she said, almost as soon as he'd closed the door. Her eyes begged for contradiction.

"Don't be silly," he hedged.

"I could never get the hang of Shakespeare," she pouted, as though it were the Bard's fault. "All those bloody words." The squall was on the horizon, he could see it mustering.

"It's all right," he lied, putting his arm around her, "you just need a little time."

Her face clouded.

197

"We open tomorrow," she said flatly. The point was difficult to refute.

"They'll tear me apart, won't they?"

He wanted to say no, but his tongue had a fit of honesty.

"Yes. Unless—"

"I'll never work again, will I? Harry talked me into this, that damn half-witted Jew: good for my reputation, he said. Bound to give me a bit more clout, he said. What does he know? Takes his ten bloody percent and leaves me holding the baby. I'm the one who looks the damn fool, aren't I?"

At the thought of looking a fool, the storm broke. No light shower this: it was a cloudburst or nothing. He did what he could, but it was difficult. She was sobbing so loudly his pearls of wisdom were drowned out. So he kissed her a little, as any decent director was bound to do, and (miracle upon miracle) that seemed to do the trick. He applied the technique with a little more gusto, his hands straying to her breasts, ferreting under her blouse for her nipples and teasing them between thumb and forefinger.

It worked wonders. There were hints of sun between the clouds now; she sniffed and unbuckled his belt, letting his heat dry out the last of the rain. His fingers were finding the lacy edge of her panties, and she was sighing as he investigated her, gently but not too gently, insistent but never too insistent. Somewhere along the line she knocked over the vodka bottle but neither of them cared to stop and right it, so it sloshed onto the floor off the edge of the table, counterpointing her instructions, his gasps.

Then the bloody door opened, and a draught blew up between them, cooling the point at issue.

Calloway almost turned around, then realized he was unbuckled, and stared instead into the mirror behind Diane to see the intruder's face. It was Lichfield. He was looking straight at Calloway, his face impassive.

"I'm sorry, I should have knocked."

His voice was as smooth as whipped cream, betraying nary a tremor of embarrassment. Calloway wedged himself away, buckled up his belt and turned to Lichfield, silently cursing his burning cheeks.

"Yes . . . it would have been polite," he said.

"Again, my apologies. I wanted a word with"—his eyes, so deep-set they were unfathomable, were on Diane— "your star," he said.

Calloway could practically feel Diane's ego expand at the word. The approach confounded him: had Lichfield undergone a volte-face? Was he coming here, the repentant admirer, to kneel at the feet of greatness?

"I would appreciate a word with the lady in private, if that were possible," the mellow voice went on.

"Well, we were just—"

"Of course," Diane interrupted. "Just allow me a moment, would you?"

She was immediately on top of the situation, tears forgotten.

"I'll be just outside," said Lichfield, already taking his leave.

Before he had closed the door behind him Diane was in front of the mirror, tissue-wrapped finger skirting her eye to divert a rivulet of mascara.

"Well," she was cooing, "how lovely to have a well-wisher. Do you know who he is?"

"His name's Lichfield," Calloway told her. "He used to be a trustee of the theater."

"Maybe he wants to offer me something."

"I doubt it."

"Oh, don't be such a drag, Terence," she snarled. "You just can't bear to have anyone else get any attention, can you?"

"My mistake."

She peered at her eyes.

"How do I look?" she asked.

"Fine."

"I'm sorry about before."

"Before?"

"You know."

"Oh . . . yes."

"I'll see you in the pub, eh?"

He was summarily dismissed apparently, his function as lover or confidant no longer required.

In the chilly corridor outside the dressing room

Lichfield was waiting patiently. Though the lights were better here than on the ill-lit stage, and he was closer now than he'd been the night before, Calloway could still not quite make out the face under the wide brim. There was something—what was the idea buzzing in his head?—something artificial about Lichfield's features. The flesh of his face didn't move as an interlocking system of muscle and tendon, it was too stiff, too pink, almost like scar-tissue.

"She's not quite ready," Calloway told him.

"She's a lovely woman," Lichfield purred.

"Yes."

"I don't blame you . . ."

"Um."

"She's no actress though."

"You're not going to interfere, are you, Lichfield? I won't let you."

"Perish the thought."

The voyeuristic pleasure Lichfield had plainly taken in his embarrassment made Calloway less respectful than he'd been.

"I won't have you upsetting her—"

"My interests are your interests, Terence. All I want to do is see this production prosper, believe me. Am I likely, under those circumstances, to alarm your Leading Lady? I'll be as meek as a lamb, Terence."

"Whatever you are," came the testy reply, "you're no lamb."

The smile appeared again on Lichfield's face, the tissue round his mouth barely stretching to accommodate his expression.

Calloway retired to the pub with that predatory sickle of teeth fixed in his mind, anxious for no reason he could focus upon.

⁂

IN THE MIRRORED CELL OF HER DRESSING ROOM Diane Duvall was just about ready to play her scene.

"You may come in now, Mr. Lichfield," she announced.

He was in the doorway before the last syllable of his name had died on her lips.

"Miss Duvall." He bowed slightly in deference to her. She smiled; so courteous. "Will you please forgive my blundering in earlier on?"

She looked coy; it always melted men.

"Mr. Calloway—" she began.

"A very insistent young man, I think."

"Yes."

"Not above pressing his attentions on his Leading Lady, perhaps?"

She frowned a little, a dancing pucker where the plucked arches of her brows converged.

"I'm afraid so."

"Most unprofessional of him," Lichfield said. "But forgive me—an understandable ardor."

She moved upstage of him, towards the lights of her mirror, and turned, knowing they would back-light her hair more flatteringly.

"Well, Mr. Lichfield, what can I do for you?"

"This is frankly a delicate matter," said Lichfield. "The bitter fact is—how shall I put this?—your talents are not ideally suited to this production. Your style lacks delicacy."

There was silence for two beats. She sniffed, thought about the inference of the remark and then moved out of center-stage towards the door. She didn't like the way this scene had begun. She was expecting an admirer, and instead she had a critic on her hands.

"Get out!" she said, her voice like slate.

"Miss Duvall—"

"You heard me."

"You're not comfortable as Viola, are you?" Lichfield continued, as though the star had said nothing.

"None of your bloody business," she spat back.

"But it is. I saw the rehearsals. You were bland, unpersuasive. The comedy is flat, the reunion scene—it should break our hearts—is leaden."

"I don't need your opinion, thank you."

"You have no style—"

"Piss off."

"No presence and no style. I'm sure on the television you are radiance itself, but the stage requires a special truth, a soulfulness you, frankly, lack."

The scene was hotting up. She wanted to hit him, but she couldn't find the proper motivation. She couldn't take this faded poseur seriously. He was more musical comedy than melodrama, with his neat grey gloves, and his neat grey cravat. Stupid, waspish queen, what did he know about acting?

"Get out before I call the Stage Manager," she said, but he stepped between her and the door.

A rape scene? Was that what they were playing? Had he got the hots for her? God forbid.

"My wife," he was saying, "has played Viola—"

"Good for her."

"—and she feels she could breathe a little more life into the role than you."

"We open tomorrow," she found herself replying, as though defending her presence. Why the hell was she trying to reason with him, barging in here and making these terrible remarks? Maybe because she was just a little afraid. His breath, close to her now, smelt of expensive chocolate.

"She knows the role by heart."

"The part's mine. And I'm doing it. I'm doing it even if I'm the worst Viola in theatrical history, all right?"

She was trying to keep her composure, but it was difficult. Something about him made her nervous. It wasn't violence she feared from him: but she feared something.

"I'm afraid I have already promised the part to my wife."

"What?" she goggled at his arrogance.

"And Constantia will play the role."

She laughed at the name. Maybe this was high comedy after all. Something from Sheridan or Wilde, arch, catty stuff. But he spoke with such absolute certainty. *Constantia will play the role*; as if it was all cut-and-dried.

"I'm not discussing this any longer, Buster, so if your wife wants to play Viola she'll have to do it in the fucking street. All right?"

"She opens tomorrow."

"Are you deaf, or stupid, or both?"

Control, an inner voice told her, you're overplaying, losing your grip on the scene. Whatever scene this is.

He stepped towards her, and the mirror lights caught the face beneath the brim full on. She hadn't looked carefully enough when he first made his appearance: now she saw the deeply etched lines, the gougings around his eyes and his mouth. It wasn't flesh, she was sure of it. He was wearing latex appliances, and they were badly glued in place. Her hand all but twitched with the desire to snatch at it and uncover his real face.

Of course. That was it. The scene she was playing: the Unmasking.

"Let's see what you look like," she said, and her hand was at his cheek before he could stop her, his smile spreading wider as she attacked. This is what he wants, she thought, but it was too late for regrets or apologies. Her fingertips had found the line of the mask at the edge

CLIVE BARKER

of his eye-socket, and curled round to take a better hold.
She yanked.

The thin veil of latex came away, and his true
physiognomy was exposed for the world to see. Diane
tried to back away, but his hand was in her hair. All she
could do was look up into that all-but-fleshless face. A
few withered strands of muscle curled here and there,
and a hint of a beard hung from a leathery flap at his
throat, but all living tissue had long since decayed. Most
of his face was simply bone: stained and worn.

"I was not," said the skull, "embalmed. Unlike
Constantia."

The explanation escaped Diane. She made no sound of
protest, which the scene would surely have justified. All
she could summon was a whimper as his hand-hold
tightened, and he hauled her head back.

"We must make a choice, sooner or later," said Lichfield,
his breath smelling less like chocolate than profound
putrescence, "between serving ourselves and serving our
art."

She didn't quite understand.

"The dead must choose more carefully than the living.
We cannot waste our breath, if you'll excuse the phrase,
on less than the purest delights. You don't want art, I
think. Do you?"

She shook her head, hoping to God that was the
expected response.

"You want the life of the body, not the life of the imagination. And you may have it."

"Thank . . . you."

"If you want it enough, you may have it."

Suddenly his hand, which had been pulling on her hair so painfully, was cupped behind her head, and bringing her lips up to meet his. She would have screamed then, as his rotting mouth fastened itself onto hers, but his greeting was so insistent it quite took her breath away.

⁜

RYAN FOUND DIANE ON THE FLOOR OF HER dressing room a few minutes before two. It was difficult to work out what had happened. There was no sign of a wound of any kind on her head or body, nor was she quite dead. She seemed to be in a coma of some kind. She had perhaps slipped, and struck her head as she fell. Whatever the cause, she was out for the count.

They were hours away from the Final Dress Rehearsal and Viola was in an ambulance, being taken in to Intensive Care.

⁜

"THE SOONER THEY KNOCK THIS PLACE DOWN, the better," said Hammersmith. He'd been drinking during office hours, something Calloway had never seen him do before. The whiskey bottle stood on his desk beside a half-full glass. There were glass-marks ringing his accounts, and his hand had a bad dose of the shakes.

"What's the news from the hospital?"

"She's a beautiful woman," he said, staring at the glass. Calloway could have sworn he was on the verge of tears.

"Hammersmith? How is she?"

"She's in a coma. But her condition is stable."

"That's something, I suppose."

Hammersmith stared up at Calloway, his erupting brows knitted in anger.

"You runt," he said, "you were screwing her, weren't you? Fancy yourself like that, don't you? Well, let me tell you something, Diane Duvall is worth a dozen of you. A dozen!"

"Is that why you let this last production go on, Hammersmith? Because you'd seen her, and you wanted to get your hot little hands on her?"

"You wouldn't understand. You've got your brain in your pants." He seemed genuinely offended by the interpretation Calloway had put on his admiration for Miss Duvall.

"All right, have it your way. We still have no Viola."

"That's why I'm canceling," said Hammersmith, slowing down to savor the moment.

It had to come. Without Diane Duvall, there would be no *Twelfth Night*; and maybe it was better that way.

208

A knock on the door.

"Who the fuck's that?" said Hammersmith softly. "Come."

It was Lichfield. Calloway was almost glad to see that strange, scarred face. Though he had a lot of questions to ask Lichfield, about the state he'd left Diane in, about their conversation together, it wasn't an interview he was willing to conduct in front of Hammersmith. Besides, any half-formed accusations he might have had were countered by the man's presence here. If Lichfield had attempted violence on Diane, for whatever reason, was it likely that he would come back so soon, so smilingly?

"Who are you?" Hammersmith demanded.

"Richard Walden Lichfield."

"I'm none the wiser."

"I used to be a trustee of the Elysium."

"Oh."

"I make it my business—"

"What do you want?" Hammersmith broke in, irritated by Lichfield's poise.

"I hear the production is in jeopardy," Lichfield replied, unruffled.

"No jeopardy," said Hammersmith, allowing himself a twitch at the corner of his mouth. "No jeopardy at all, because there's no show. It's been canceled."

"Oh?" Lichfield looked at Calloway.

"Is this with your consent?" he asked.

"He has no say in the matter; I have sole right of

cancellation if circumstances dictate it; it's in his contract. The theater is closed as of today; it will not reopen."

"Yes it will," said Lichfield.

"What?" Hammersmith stood up behind his desk, and Calloway realized he'd never seen the man standing before. He was very short.

"We will play *Twelfth Night* as advertised," Lichfield purred. "My wife has kindly agreed to understudy the part of Viola in place of Miss Duvall."

Hammersmith laughed, a coarse, butcher's laugh. It died on his lips however, as the office was suffused with lavender, and Constantia Lichfield made her entrance, shimmering in silk and fur. She looked as perfect as the day she died: even Hammersmith held his breath and his silence at the sight of her.

"Our new Viola," Lichfield announced.

After a moment Hammersmith found his voice. "This woman can't step in at half a day's notice."

"Why not?" said Calloway, not taking his eyes off the woman. Lichfield was a lucky man; Constantia was an extraordinary beauty. He scarcely dared draw breath in her presence for fear she'd vanish.

Then she spoke. The lines were from Act V, Scene I:

"If nothing lets to make us happy both
But this my masculine usurp'd attire,
Do not embrace me 'til each circumstance
Of place, time, fortune, do cohere and jump
That I am Viola."

The voice was light and musical, but it seemed to resound in her body, filling each phrase with an undercurrent of suppressed passion.

And that face. It was wonderfully alive, the features playing the story of her speech with delicate economy.

She was enchanting.

"I'm sorry," said Hammersmith, "but there are rules and regulations about this sort of thing. Is she Equity?"

"No," said Lichfield.

"Well you see, it's impossible. The Union strictly precludes this kind of thing. They'd flay us alive."

"What's it to you, Hammersmith?" said Calloway. "What the fuck do you care? You'll never need set foot in a theater again once this place is demolished."

"My wife has watched the rehearsals. She is word perfect."

"It could be magic," said Calloway, his enthusiasm firing up with every moment he looked at Constantia.

"You're risking the Union, Calloway," Hammersmith chided.

"I'll take the risk."

"As you say, it's nothing to me. But if a little bird was to tell them, you'd have egg on your face."

"Hammersmith: give her a chance. Give all of us a chance. If Equity blacks me, that's my look-out." Hammersmith sat down again.

"Nobody'll come, you know that, don't you? Diane Duvall was a star; they would have sat through your turgid production to see her, Calloway. But an unknown . . . ? Well, it's your funeral. Go ahead and do it, I wash my hands of the whole thing. It's on your head, Calloway, remember that. I hope they flay you for it."

"Thank you," said Lichfield. "Most kind."

Hammersmith began to rearrange his desk, to give more prominence to the bottle and the glass. The interview was over: he wasn't interested in these butterflies any longer.

"Go away," he said. "Just go away."

⁂

"I HAVE ONE OR TWO REQUESTS TO MAKE," Lichfield told Calloway as they left the office. "Alterations to the production which would enhance my wife's performance."

"What are they?"

"For Constantia's comfort, I would ask that the lighting levels be taken down substantially. She's simply not accustomed to performing under such hot, bright lights."

"Very well."

"I'd also request that we install a row of footlights."

"Footlights?"

"An odd requirement, I realize, but she feels much happier with footlights."

"They tend to dazzle the actors," said Calloway. "It becomes difficult to see the audience."

"Nevertheless . . . I have to stipulate their installation."

"OK."

"Thirdly—I would ask that all scenes involving kissing, embracing or otherwise touching Constantia be redirected to remove every instance of physical contact whatsoever."

"Everything?"

"Everything."

"For God's sake why?"

"My wife needs no business to dramatize the working of the heart, Terence."

That curious intonation on the word "heart." Working of the *heart*.

Calloway caught Constantia's eye for the merest of moments. It was like being blessed.

"Shall we introduce our new Viola to the company?" Lichfield suggested.

"Why not?"

The trio went into the theater.

⚜

THE REARRANGING OF THE BLOCKING AND THE business to exclude any physical contact was simple. And though the rest of the cast were initially wary of their new colleague, her unaffected manner and her natural grace soon had them at her feet. Besides, her presence meant that the show would go on.

✢

AT SIX, CALLOWAY CALLED A BREAK, ANNOUNCING that they'd begin the Dress at eight, and telling them to go out and enjoy themselves for an hour or so. The company went their ways, buzzing with a newfound enthusiasm for the production. What had looked like a shambles half a day earlier now seemed to be shaping up quite well. There were a thousand things to be sniped at, of course: technical shortcomings, costumes that fitted badly, directorial foibles. All par for the course. In fact, the actors were happier than they'd been in a good while. Even Ed Cunningham was not above passing a compliment or two.

✢

LICHFIELD FOUND TALLULAH IN THE GREEN Room, tidying.

"Tonight . . ."

"Yes, sir."

"You must not be afraid."

"I'm not afraid," Tallulah replied. "What a thought. As if—"

"There may be some pain, which I regret. For you, indeed for all of us."

"I understand."

"Of course you do. You love the theater as I love it: you know the paradox of this profession. To play life . . .

214

ah, Tallulah, to play life . . . what a curious thing it is. Sometimes I wonder, you know, how long I can keep up the illusion."

"It's a wonderful performance," she said.

"Do you think so? Do you really think so?" He was encouraged by her favorable review. It was so galling, to have to pretend all the time; to fake the flesh, the breath, the look of life. Grateful for Tallulah's opinion, he reached for her.

"Would you like to die, Tallulah?"

"Does it hurt?"

"Scarcely at all."

"It would make me very happy."

"And so it should."

His mouth covered her mouth, and she was dead in less than a minute, conceding happily to his inquiring tongue. He laid her out on the threadbare couch and locked the door of the Green Room with her own key. She'd cool easily in the chill of the room, and be up and about again by the time the audience arrived.

⁜

AT SIX-FIFTEEN DIANE DUVALL GOT OUT OF A taxi at the front of the Elysium. It was well dark, a windy November night, but she felt fine; nothing could depress tonight. Not the dark, not the cold.

Unseen, she made her way past the posters that bore

215

her face and name, and through the empty auditorium to her dressing room. There, smoking his way through a pack of cigarettes, she found the object of her affection.

"Terry."

She posed in the doorway for a moment, letting the fact of her reappearance sink in. He went quite white at the sight of her, so she pouted a little. It wasn't easy to pout. There was a stiffness in the muscles of her face but she carried off the effect to her satisfaction.

Calloway was lost for words. Diane looked ill, no two ways about it, and if she'd left the hospital to take up her part in the Dress Rehearsal he was going to have to convince her otherwise. She was wearing no makeup, and her ash-blond hair needed a wash.

"What are you doing here?" he asked, as she closed the door behind her.

"Unfinished business," she said.

"Listen . . . I've got something to tell you . . ."

God, this was going to be messy. "We've found a replacement, in the show." She looked at him blankly. He hurried on, tripping over his own words. "We thought you were out of commission, I mean, not permanently, but, you know, for the opening at least . . ."

"Don't worry," she said.

His jaw dropped a little.

"Don't worry?"

"What's it to me?"

"You said you came back to finish—"

He stopped. She was unbuttoning the top of her dress. She's not serious, he thought, she can't be serious. Sex? Now?

"I've done a lot of thinking in the last few hours," she said as she shimmied the crumpled dress over her hips, let it fall and stepped out of it. She was wearing a white bra, which she tried, unsuccessfully, to unhook. "I've decided I don't care about the theater. Help me, will you?"

She turned round and presented her back to him. Automatically he unhooked the bra, not really analyzing whether he wanted this or not. It seemed to be a *fait accompli*. She'd come back to finish what they'd been interrupted doing, simple as that. And despite the bizarre noises she was making in the back of her throat, and the glassy look in her eyes, she was still an attractive woman. She turned again, and Calloway stared at the fullness of her breasts, paler than he'd remembered them, but lovely. His trousers were becoming uncomfortably tight, and her performance was only worsening his situation, the way she was grinding her hips like the rawest of Soho strippers, running her hands between her legs.

"Don't worry about me," she said, "I've made up my mind. All I really want . . ."

She put her hands, so recently at her groin, on his face. They were icy cold.

"All I really want is you. I can't have sex *and* the stage . . . There comes a time in everyone's life when decisions have to be made."

She licked her lips. There was no film of moisture left on her mouth when her tongue had passed over it.

"The accident made me think, made me analyze what it is I really care about. And frankly"—she was unbuckling his belt—"I don't give a shit—"

Now the zip.

"—about this, or any other fucking play."

His trousers fell down.

"I'll show you what I care about."

She reached into his briefs, and clasped him. Her cold hand somehow made the touch sexier. He laughed, closing his eyes as she pulled his briefs down to the middle of his thigh and knelt at his feet.

She was as expert as ever, her throat open like a drain. Her mouth was somewhat drier than usual, her tongue scouring him, but the sensations drove him wild. It was so good, he scarcely noticed the ease with which she devoured him, taking him deeper than she'd ever managed previously, using every trick she knew to goad him higher and higher. Slow and deep, then picking up speed until he almost came, then slowing again until the need passed. He was completely at her mercy.

He opened his eyes to watch her at work. She was skewering herself upon him, face in rapture.

"God," he gasped, "that is *so* good. Oh yes, oh yes."

Her face didn't even flicker in response to his words, she just continued to work at him soundlessly. She wasn't making her usual noises, the small grunts of satisfaction, the heavy breathing through the nose. She just ate his flesh in absolute silence.

He held his breath a moment, while an idea was born in his belly. The bobbing head bobbed on, eyes closed, lips clamped around his member, utterly engrossed. Half a minute passed; a minute; a minute and a half. And now his belly was full of terrors.

She wasn't breathing. She was giving this matchless blow-job because she wasn't stopping, even for a moment, to inhale or exhale.

Calloway felt his body go rigid, while his erection wilted in her throat. She didn't falter in her labor; the relentless pumping continued at his groin even as his mind formed the unthinkable thought:

She's dead.

She has me in her mouth, in her cold mouth, and she's dead. That's why she'd come back, got up off her mortuary slab and come back. She was eager to finish what she'd started, no longer caring about the play, or her usurper. It was this act she valued, this act alone. She'd chosen to perform it for eternity.

Calloway could do nothing with the realization but stare down like a damn fool while this corpse gave him head.

Then it seemed she sensed his horror. She opened her eyes and looked up at him. How could he ever have mistaken that dead stare for life? Gently, she withdrew his shrunken manhood from between her lips.

"What is it?" she asked, her fluting voice still affecting life.

"You . . . you're not . . . breathing."

Her face fell. She let him go.

"Oh, darling," she said, letting all pretense to life disappear, "I'm not so good at playing the part, am I?"

Her voice was a ghost's voice: thin, forlorn. Her skin, which he had thought so flatteringly pale, was, on second view, a waxen white.

"You are dead?" he said.

"I'm afraid so. Two hours ago: in my sleep. But I had to come, Terry; so much unfinished business. I made my choice. You should be flattered. You are flattered, aren't you?"

She stood up and reached into her handbag, which she'd left beside the mirror. Calloway looked at the door, trying to make his limbs work, but they were inert. Besides, he had his trousers round his ankles. Two steps and he'd fall flat on his face.

She turned back on him, with something silver and sharp in her hand. Try as he might, he couldn't get a focus on it. But whatever it was, she meant it for him.

❖

SINCE THE BUILDING OF THE NEW CREMATORIUM in 1934, one humiliation had come after another for the cemetery. The tombs had been raided for lead coffin-linings, the stones overturned and smashed; it was fouled by dogs and graffiti. Very few mourners now came to tend the graves. The generations had dwindled, and the small number of people who might still have had a loved one buried there were too infirm to risk the throttled walkways, or too tender to bear looking at such vandalism.

It had not always been so. There were illustrious and influential families interred behind the marble façades of the Victorian mausoleums. Founder fathers, local industrialists and dignitaries, any and all who had done the town proud by their efforts. The body of the actress Constantia Lichfield had been buried here ("Until the Day Break and the Shadows Flee Away"), though her grave was almost unique in the attention some secret admirer still paid to it.

Nobody was watching that night, it was too bitter for lovers. Nobody saw Charlotte Hancock open the door of her sepulcher, with the beating wings of pigeons applauding her vigor as she shambled out to meet the moon. Her husband, Gerard, was with her, he less fresh than she, having been dead thirteen years longer. Joseph Jardine, *en famille*, was not far behind the Hancocks, as was Marriott Fletcher, and Anne Snell, and the Peacock Brothers; the list went on and on. In one corner, Alfred Crawshaw (Captain in the 17th Lancers), was helping his lovely wife, Emma, from the rot of their bed. Everywhere faces pressed at the cracks of the tomb lids—was that not Kezia Reynolds with her child, who'd lived just a day, in her arms; and Martin van de Linde (the Memory of the Just is Blessed), whose wife had never been found; Rosa and Selina Goldfinch: upstanding women both; and Thomas Jerrey, and—?

Too many names to mention. Too many states of decay to describe. Sufficient to say they rose: their burial finery flyborn, their faces stripped of all but the foundation of beauty. Still they came, swinging open the back gate of the cemetery and threading their way across the wasteland towards the Elysium. In the distance, the sound of traffic. Above, a jet roared in to land. One of the Peacock brothers, staring up at the winking giant as it passed over, missed his footing and fell on his face, shattering his jaw. They picked him up fondly, and escorted him on his way. There was no harm done; and what would a resurrection be without a few laughs?

⊰⊱

So THE SHOW WENT ON.

"If music be the food of love, play on,
  Give me excess of it; that, surfeiting,
  The appetite may sicken and so die—"

Calloway could not be found at Curtain; but Ryan had instructions from Hammersmith (through the ubiquitous Mr. Lichfield) to take the show up with or without the Director.

"He'll be upstairs, in the Gods," said Lichfield. "In fact, I think I can see him from here."

"Is he smiling?" asked Eddie.

"Grinning from ear to ear."

"Then he's pissed."

The actors laughed. There was a good deal of laughter that night. The show was running smoothly, and though they couldn't see the audience over the glare of the newly installed footlights they could feel the waves of love and delight pouring out of the auditorium. The actors were coming off stage elated.

"They're all sitting in the Gods," said Eddie, "but your friends, Mr. Lichfield, do an old ham good. They're quiet of course, but such big smiles on their faces."

Act I, Scene II; and the first entrance of Constantia Lichfield as Viola was met with spontaneous applause. Such applause. Like the hollow roll of snare drums, like the brittle beating of a thousand sticks on a thousand stretched skins. Lavish, wanton applause.

And, my God, she rose to the occasion. She began the play as she meant to go on, giving her whole heart to the role, not needing physicality to communicate the depth of her feelings, but speaking the poetry with such intelligence and passion the merest flutter of her hand was worth more than a hundred grander gestures. After that first scene her every entrance was met with the same applause from the audience, followed by almost reverential silence.

Backstage, a kind of buoyant confidence had set in. The whole company sniffed the success; a success which had been snatched miraculously from the jaws of disaster.

There again! Applause! Applause!

❧

IN HIS OFFICE, HAMMERSMITH DIMLY registered the brittle din of adulation through a haze of booze.

He was in the act of pouring his eighth drink when the door opened. He glanced up for a moment and registered that the visitor was that upstart Calloway. Come to gloat I daresay, Hammersmith thought, come to tell me how wrong I was.

"What do you want?"

The punk didn't answer. From the corner of his eye Hammersmith had an impression of a broad, bright smile on Calloway's face. Self-satisfied half-wit, coming in here when a man was in mourning.

"I suppose you've heard?"

The other grunted.

"She died," said Hammersmith, beginning to cry. "She died a few hours ago, without regaining consciousness. I haven't told the actors. Didn't seem worth it."

Calloway said nothing in reply to this news. Didn't the bastard care? Couldn't he see that this was the end of the world? The woman was dead. She'd died in the bowels of the Elysium. There'd be official inquiries made, the insurance would be examined, a postmortem, an inquest: it would reveal too much.

He drank deeply from his glass, not bothering to look at Calloway again.

"Your career'll take a dive after this, son. It won't just be me: oh dear no."

Still Calloway kept his silence.

"Don't you care?" Hammersmith demanded.

There was silence for a moment, then Calloway responded. "I don't give a shit."

"Jumped-up little stage-manager, that's all you are. That's all *any* of you fucking directors are! One good review and you're God's gift to art. Well let me set you straight about that—"

He looked at Calloway, his eyes, swimming in alcohol, having difficulty focussing. But he got there eventually.

Calloway, the dirty bugger, was naked from the waist down. He was wearing his shoes and his socks, but no trousers or briefs. His self-exposure would have been comical, but for the expression on his face. The man had gone mad: his eyes were rolling around uncontrollably, saliva and snot ran from mouth and nose, his tongue hung out like the tongue of a panting dog.

Hammersmith put his glass down on his blotting pad, and looked at the worst part. There was blood on Calloway's shirt, a trail of it which led up his neck to his left ear, from which protruded the end of Diane Duvall's nail-file. It had been driven deep into Calloway's brain. The man was surely dead.

But he stood, spoke, walked.

From the theater, there rose another round of applause, muted by distance. It wasn't a real sound somehow; it came from another world, a place where emotions ruled. It was a world Hammersmith had always felt excluded from. He'd never been much of an actor, though God knows he'd tried, and the two plays he'd penned were, he knew, execrable. Bookkeeping was his forte, and he'd used it to stay as close to the stage as he could, hating his own lack of art as much as he resented that skill in others.

The applause died, and as if taking a cue from an unseen prompter, Calloway came at him. The mask he wore was neither comic nor tragic, it was blood and laughter together. Cowering, Hammersmith was cornered behind his desk. Calloway leapt onto it (he looked so ridiculous, shirt-tails and balls flip-flapping) and seized Hammersmith by the tie.

"Philistine," said Calloway, never now to know Hammersmith's heart, and broke the man's neck—snap!—while below the applause began again.

❧

"DO NOT EMBRACE ME 'TIL EACH CIRCUMSTANCE
  Of place, time, fortune, do cohere and jump

That I am Viola."

From Constantia's mouth the lines were a revelation. It was almost as though this *Twelfth Night* were a new play, and the part of Viola had been written for Constantia Lichfield alone. The actors who shared the stage with her felt their egos shriveling in the face of such a gift.

The last act continued to its bittersweet conclusion, the audience as enthralled as ever to judge by their breathless attention.

The Duke spoke: "Give me thy hand;

And let me see thee in thy woman's weeds."

In the rehearsal the invitation in the line had been ignored: no one was to touch this Viola, much less take her hand. But in the heat of the performance such taboos were forgotten. Possessed by the passion of the moment the actor reached for Constantia. She, forgetting the taboo in her turn, reached to answer his touch.

In the wings Lichfield breathed "no" under his breath, but his order wasn't heard. The Duke grasped Viola's hand in his, life and death holding court together under this painted sky.

It was a chilly hand, a hand without blood in its veins, or a blush in its skin.

But here it was as good as alive.

They were equals, the living and the dead, and nobody could find just cause to part them.

In the wings Lichfield sighed, and allowed himself a smile. He'd feared that touch, feared it would break the spell. But Dionysus was with them tonight. All would be well; he felt it in his bones.

The act drew to a close, and Malvolio, still trumpeting his threats, even in defeat, was carted off. One by one the company exited, leaving the clown to wrap up the play.

"A great while ago the world begun,

With hey, ho, the wind and the rain,

But that's all one, our play is done

And we'll strive to please you every day."

The scene darkened to blackout, and the curtain descended. From the Gods rapturous applause erupted, that same rattling, hollow applause. The company, their faces shining with the success of the Dress Rehearsal, formed behind the curtain for the bow. The curtain rose: the applause mounted.

In the wings, Calloway joined Lichfield. He was dressed now: and he'd washed the blood off his neck.

"Well, we have a brilliant success," said the skull. "It does seem a pity that this company should be dissolved so soon."

"It does," said the corpse.

The actors were shouting into the wings now, calling for Calloway to join them. They were applauding him, encouraging him to show his face.

He put a hand on Lichfield's shoulder.

"We'll go together, sir," he said.

"No, no, I couldn't."

"You must. It's your triumph as much as mine."

Lichfield nodded, and they went out together to take their bows beside the company.

⁕

IN THE WINGS TALLULAH WAS AT WORK. SHE felt restored after her sleep in the Green Room. So much unpleasantness had gone, taken with her life. She no longer suffered the aches in her hip, or the creeping neuralgia in her scalp. There was no longer the necessity to draw breath through pipes encrusted with seventy years' muck, or to rub the backs of her hands to get the circulation going; not even the need to blink. She laid the fires with a new strength, pressing the detritus of past productions into use: old backdrops, props, costuming. When she had enough combustibles heaped, she struck a match and set the flame to them. The Elysium began to burn.

⁕

OVER THE APPLAUSE, SOMEBODY WAS SHOUTING:
"Marvelous, sweethearts, marvelous."
It was Diane's voice, they all recognized it even though they couldn't quite see her. She was staggering down the center aisle towards the stage, making quite a fool of herself.
"Silly bitch," said Eddie.
"Whoops," said Calloway.

She was at the edge of the stage now, haranguing him.

"Got all you wanted now, have you? This your new lady-love, is it? Is it?"

She was trying to clamber up, her hands gripping the hot metal hoods of the footlights. Her skin began to singe: the fat was well and truly in the fire.

"For God's sake, somebody stop her," said Eddie. But she didn't seem to feel the searing of her hands; she just laughed in his face. The smell of burning flesh wafted up from the footlights. The company broke rank, triumph forgotten.

Somebody yelled: "Kill the lights!"

A beat, and then the stage lights were extinguished. Diane fell back, her hands smoking. One of the cast fainted, another ran into the wings to be sick. Somewhere behind them, they could hear the faint crackle of flames, but they had other calls on their attention.

With the footlights gone, they could see the auditorium more clearly. The stalls were empty, but the Balcony and the Gods were full to bursting with eager admirers. Every row was packed, and every available inch of aisle space thronged with audience. Somebody up there started clapping again, alone for a few moments before the wave of applause began afresh. But now few of the company took pride in it.

Even from the stage, even with exhausted and light-dazzled eyes, it was obvious that no man, woman or child in that adoring crowd was alive. They waved fine silk handkerchiefs at the players in rotted fists, some of them beat a tattoo on the seats in front of them, most just clapped, bone on bone.

Calloway smiled, bowed deeply and received their admiration and gratitude. In all his fifteen years of work in the theater he had never found an audience so appreciative.

Bathing in the love of their admirers, Constantia and Richard Lichfield joined hands and walked down-stage to take another bow, while the living actors retreated in horror.

They began to yell and pray, they let out howls, they ran about like discovered adulterers in a farce. But, like the farce, there was no way out of the situation. There were bright flames tickling the roof-joists, and billows of canvas cascaded down to right and left as the flies caught fire. In front, the dead: behind, death. Smoke was beginning to thicken the air, it was impossible to see where one was going. Somebody was wearing a toga of burning canvas, and reciting screams. Someone else was wielding a fire extinguisher against the inferno. All useless: all tired business, badly managed. As the roof began to give, lethal falls of timber and girder silenced most.

In the Gods, the audience had more or less departed. They were ambling back to their graves long before the fire department appeared, their cerements and their faces lit by the glow of the fire as they glanced over their shoulders to watch the Elysium perish. It had been a fine show, and they were happy to go home, content for another while to gossip in the dark.

✢

THE FIRE BURNED THROUGH THE NIGHT, despite the never less than gallant efforts of the fire department to put it out. By four in the morning the fight was given up as lost, and the conflagration allowed its head. It had done with the Elysium by dawn.

In the ruins the remains of several persons were discovered, most of the bodies in states that defied easy identification. Dental records were consulted, and one corpse was found to be that of Giles Hammersmith (Administrator), another that of Ryan Xavier (Stage Manager) and, most shockingly, a third that of Diane Duvall. "Star of *The Love Child* burned to death," read the tabloids. She was forgotten in a week.

There were no survivors. Several bodies were simply never found.

✢

THEY STOOD AT THE SIDE OF THE MOTORWAY, and watched the cars careering through the night.

Lichfield was there of course, and Constantia, radiant

as ever. Calloway had chosen to go with them, so had Eddie, and Tallulah. Three or four others had also joined the troupe.

It was the first night of their freedom, and here they were on the open road, traveling players. The smoke alone had killed Eddie, but there were a few more serious injuries amongst their number, sustained in the fire. Burned bodies, broken limbs. But the audience they would play for in the future would forgive them their petty mutilations.

"There are lives lived for love," said Lichfield to his new company, "and lives lived for art. We happy band have chosen the latter persuasion."

There was a ripple of applause amongst the actors.

"To you, who have never died, may I say: welcome to the world!"

Laughter: further applause.

The lights of the cars racing north along the motorway threw the company into silhouette. They looked, to all intents and purposes, like living men and women. But then wasn't that the trick of their craft? To imitate life so well the illusion was indistinguishable from the real thing? And their new public, awaiting them in mortuaries, churchyards and chapels of rest, would appreciate that skill more than most. Who better to applaud the sham of passion and pain they would perform than the dead, who had experienced such feelings, and thrown them off at last?

233

The dead. They needed entertainment no less than the living; and they were a sorely neglected market.

Not that this company would perform for money, they would play for the love of their art, Lichfield had made that clear from the outset. No more service would be done to Apollo.

"Now," he said, "which road shall we take, north or south?"

"North," said Eddie. "My mother's buried in Glasgow, she died before I ever played professionally. I'd like her to see me."

"North it is, then," said Lichfield. "Shall we go and find ourselves some transport?"

He led the way towards the motorway restaurant, its neon flickering fitfully, keeping the night at light's length. The colors were theatrically bright: scarlet, lime, cobalt and a wash of white that splashed out of the windows onto the car park where they stood. The automatic doors hissed as a traveler emerged, bearing gifts of hamburgers and cake to the child in the back of his car.

"Surely some friendly driver will find a niche for us," said Lichfield.

"All of us?" said Calloway.

"A truck will do; beggars can't be too demanding," said Lichfield. "And we are beggars now: subject to the whim of our patrons."

"We can always steal a car," said Tallulah.

234

"No need for theft, except in extremity," Lichfield said. "Constantia and I will go ahead and find a chauffeur."

He took his wife's hand.

"Nobody refuses beauty," he said.

"What do we do if anyone asks us what we're doing here?" asked Eddie nervously. He wasn't used to this role; he needed reassurance.

Lichfield turned towards the company, his voice booming in the night:

"What do you do?" he said. "Play life, of course! And smile!"

IN THE HILLS,
THE CITIES

I T WASN'T UNTIL THE FIRST WEEK OF THE
Yugoslavian trip that Mick discovered what a political
bigot he'd chosen as a lover. Certainly, he'd been warned.
One of the queens at the Baths had told him Judd was to
the Right of Attila the Hun, but the man had been one
of Judd's ex-affairs, and Mick had presumed there was
more spite than perception in the character assassination.

If only he'd listened. Then he wouldn't be driving
along an interminable road in a Volkswagen that suddenly
seemed the size of a coffin, listening to Judd's views on
Soviet expansionism. Jesus, he was so boring. He didn't
converse, he lectured, and endlessly. In Italy the sermon

had been on the way the Communists had exploited the peasant vote. Now, in Yugoslavia, Judd had really warmed to this theme, and Mick was just about ready to take a hammer to his self-opinionated head.

It wasn't that he disagreed with everything Judd said. Some of the arguments (the ones Mick understood) seemed quite sensible. But then, what did he know? He was a dance teacher. Judd was a journalist, a professional pundit. He felt, like most journalists Mick had encountered, that he was obliged to have an opinion on everything under the sun. Especially politics; that was the best trough to wallow in. You could get your snout, eyes, head and front hooves in that mess of muck and have a fine old time splashing around. It was an inexhaustible subject to devour, a swill with a little of everything in it, because everything, according to Judd, was political. The arts were political. Sex was political. Religion, commerce, gardening, eating, drinking and farting—all political.

Jesus, it was mind-blowingly boring; killingly, love-deadeningly boring.

Worse still, Judd didn't seem to notice how bored Mick had become, or if he noticed, he didn't care. He just rambled on, his arguments getting windier and windier, his sentences lengthening with every mile they drove.

Judd, Mick had decided, was a selfish bastard, and as soon as their honeymoon was over he'd part with the guy.

❖

IT WAS NOT UNTIL THEIR TRIP, THAT ENDLESS, motiveless caravan through the graveyards of mid-European culture, that Judd realized what a political lightweight he had in Mick. The guy showed precious little interest in the economics or the politics of the countries they passed through. He registered indifference to the full facts behind the Italian situation, and yawned, yes, yawned when he tried (and failed) to debate the Russian threat to world peace. He had to face the bitter truth: Mick was a queen; there was no other word for him; all right, perhaps he didn't mince or wear jewelry to excess, but he was a queen nevertheless, happy to wallow in a dreamworld of early Renaissance frescoes and Yugoslavian icons. The complexities, the contradictions, even the agonies that made those cultures blossom and wither were just tiresome to him. His mind was no deeper than his looks; he was a well-groomed nobody.

Some honeymoon.

❖

THE ROAD SOUTH FROM BELGRADE TO NOVI Pazar was, by Yugoslavian standards, a good one. There were fewer potholes than on many of the roads they'd traveled, and it was relatively straight. The town of Novi Pazar lay in the valley of the River Raska, south of the city named after the river. It wasn't an area particularly popular with the tourists. Despite the good road it was still inaccessible, and lacked sophisticated amenities; but Mick was determined to see the monastery at Sopocani, to the west of the town, and after some bitter argument, he'd won.

The journey had proved uninspiring. On either side of the road the cultivated fields looked parched and dusty. The summer had been unusually hot, and droughts were affecting many of the villages. Crops had failed, and livestock had been prematurely slaughtered to prevent them dying of malnutrition. There was a defeated look about the few faces they glimpsed at the roadside. Even the children had dour expressions; brows as heavy as the stale heat that hung over the valley.

Now, with the cards on the table after a row at Belgrade, they drove in silence most of the time; but the straight road, like most straight roads, invited dispute. When the driving was easy, the mind rooted for something to keep it engaged. What better than a fight?

"Why the hell do you want to see this damn monastery?" Judd demanded.

It was an unmistakable invitation.

"We've come all this way . . ." Mick tried to keep the tone conversational. He wasn't in the mood for an argument.

"More fucking Virgins, is it?"

Keeping his voice as even as he could, Mick picked up

the guide and read aloud from it: ". . . there, some of the greatest works of Serbian painting can still be seen and enjoyed, including what many commentators agree to be the enduring masterpiece of the Raska school: the Dormition of the Virgin."

Silence.

Then Judd: "I'm up to here with churches."

"It's a masterpiece."

"They're all masterpieces according to that bloody book."

Mick felt his control slipping.

"Two and a half hours at most—"

"I told you, I don't want to see another church; the smell of the places makes me sick. Stale incense, old sweat and lies . . ."

"It's a short detour; then we can get back onto the road and you can give me another lecture on farming subsidies in the Sandzak."

"I'm just trying to get some decent conversation going instead of this endless tripe about Serbian fucking masterpieces—"

"Stop the car!"

"What?"

"Stop the car!"

Judd pulled the Volkswagen into the side of the road. Mick got out.

The road was hot, but there was a slight breeze. He took a deep breath, and wandered into the middle of the road. Empty of traffic and of pedestrians in both directions. In every direction, empty. The hills shimmered in the heat off the fields. There were wild poppies growing in the ditches. Mick crossed the road, squatted on his haunches and picked one.

Behind him he heard the VW's door slam.

"What did you stop us for?" Judd said. His voice was edgy, still hoping for that argument, begging for it.

Mick stood up, playing with the poppy. It was close to seeding, late in the season. The petals fell from the receptacle as soon as he touched them, little splashes of red fluttering down onto the grey tarmac.

"I asked you a question," Judd said.

Mick looked around. Judd was standing at the far side of the car, his brows a knitted line of burgeoning anger. But handsome; oh yes; a face that made women weep with frustration that he was gay. A heavy black moustache (perfectly trimmed) and eyes you could watch forever and never see the same light in them twice. Why in God's name, thought Mick, does a man as fine as that have to be such an insensitive little shit?

Judd returned the look of contemptuous appraisal, staring at the pouting pretty boy across the road. It made him want to puke, seeing the little act Mick was performing for his benefit. It might just have been plausible in a sixteen-year-old virgin. In a twenty-five-year-old, it lacked credibility.

Mick dropped the flower, and untucked his T-shirt

244

from his jeans. A tight stomach, then a slim, smooth chest were revealed as he pulled it off. His hair was ruffled when his head reappeared, and his face wore a broad grin. Judd looked at the torso. Neat, not too muscular. An appendix scar peering over his faded jeans. A gold chain, small but catching the sun, dipped in the hollow of his throat. Without meaning to, he returned Mick's grin, and a kind of peace was made between them.

Mick was unbuckling his belt.

"Want to fuck?" he said, the grin not faltering.

"It's no use," came an answer, though not to that question.

"What isn't?"

"We're not compatible."

"Want to bet?"

Now he was unzipped, and turning away towards the wheat field that bordered the road.

Judd watched as Mick cut a swath through the swaying sea, his back the color of the grain, so that he was almost camouflaged by it. It was a dangerous game, screwing in the open air—this wasn't San Francisco, or even Hampstead Heath. Nervously, Judd glanced along the road. Still empty in both directions. And Mick was turning, deep in the field, turning and smiling and waving like a swimmer buoyed up in a golden surf. What the hell? . . . There was nobody to see, nobody to know. Just the hills, liquid in the heat-haze, their forested backs bent to the business of the earth, and a lost dog, sitting at the edge of the road, waiting for some lost master.

Judd followed Mick's path through the wheat, unbuttoning his shirt as he walked. Field mice ran ahead of him, scurrying through the stalks as the giant came their way, his feet like thunder. Judd saw their panic, and smiled. He meant no harm to them, but then how were they to know that? Maybe he'd put out a hundred lives, mice, beetles, worms, before he reached the spot where Mick was lying, stark bollock naked, on a bed of trampled grain, still grinning.

It was good love they made, good, strong love, equal in pleasure for both; there was a precision to their passion, sensing the moment when effortless delight became urgent, when desire became necessity. They locked together, limb around limb, tongue around tongue, in a knot only orgasm could untie, their backs alternately scorched and scratched as they rolled around exchanging blows and kisses. In the thick of it, creaming together, they heard the phut-phut-phut of a tractor passing by; but they were past caring.

They made their way back to the Volkswagen with body-threshed wheat in their hair and their ears, in their socks and between their toes. Their grins had been replaced with easy smiles: the truce, if not permanent, would last a few hours at least.

The car was baking hot, and they had to open all the windows and doors to let the breeze cool it before they started towards Novi Pazar. It was four o'clock, and there was still an hour's driving ahead.

As they got into the car Mick said, "We'll forget the monastery, eh?"

Judd gaped.

"I thought—"

"I couldn't bear another fucking Virgin—"

They laughed lightly together, then kissed, tasting each other and themselves, a mingling of saliva and the aftertaste of salt semen.

THE FOLLOWING DAY WAS BRIGHT, BUT NOT particularly warm. No blue skies: just an even layer of white cloud. The morning air was sharp in the lining of the nostrils, like ether, or peppermint.

Vaslav Jelovsek watched the pigeons in the main square of Popolac courting death as they skipped and fluttered ahead of the vehicles that were buzzing around. Some about military business, some civilian. An air of sober intention barely suppressed the excitement he felt on this day, an excitement he knew was shared by every man, woman and child in Popolac. Shared by the pigeons too for all he knew. Maybe that was why they played under the wheels with such dexterity, knowing that on this day of days no harm could come to them.

He scanned the sky again, that same white sky he'd

been peering at since dawn. The cloud-layer was low; not ideal for the celebrations. A phrase passed through his mind, an English phrase he'd heard from a friend, "to have your head in the clouds." It meant, he gathered, to be lost in a reverie, in a white, sightless dream. That, he thought wryly, was all the West knew about clouds, that they stood for dreams. It took a vision they lacked to make a truth out of that casual turn of phrase. Here, in these secret hills, wouldn't they create a spectacular reality from those idle words? A living proverb.

A head in the clouds.

Already the first contingent was assembling in the square. There were one or two absentees owing to illness, but the auxiliaries were ready and waiting to take their places. Such eagerness! Such wide smiles when an auxiliary heard his or her name and number called and was taken out of line to join the limb that was already taking shape. On every side, miracles of organization. Everyone with a job to do and a place to go. There was no shouting or pushing: indeed, voices were scarcely raised above an eager whisper. He watched in admiration as the work of positioning and buckling and roping went on.

It was going to be a long and arduous day. Vaslav had been in the square since an hour before dawn, drinking coffee from imported plastic cups, discussing the half-hourly meteorological reports coming in from Pristina and Mitrovica, and watching the starless sky as the grey light of morning crept across it. Now he was drinking his sixth coffee of the day, and it was still barely seven o'clock. Across the square Metzinger looked as tired and as anxious as Vaslav felt.

They'd watched the dawn seep out of the east together. Metzinger and he. But now they had separated, forgetting previous companionship, and would not speak until the contest was over. After all, Metzinger was from Podujevo. He had his own city to support in the coming battle. Tomorrow they'd exchange tales of their adventures, but for today they must behave as if they didn't know each other, not even to exchange a smile. For today they had to be utterly partisan, caring only for the victory of their own city over the opposition.

Now the first leg of Popolac was erected, to the mutual satisfaction of Metzinger and Vaslav. All the safety checks had been meticulously made, and the leg left the square, its shadow falling hugely across the face of the Town Hall.

Vaslav sipped his sweet, sweet coffee and allowed himself a little grunt of satisfaction. Such days, such days. Days filled with glory, with snapping flags and high, stomach-turning sights, enough to last a man a lifetime. It was a golden foretaste of Heaven.

Let America have its simple pleasures, its cartoon mice, its candy-coated castles, its cults and its technologies, he wanted none of it. The greatest wonder of the world was here, hidden in the hills.

Ah, such days.

In the main square of Podujevo the scene was no less animated, and no less inspiring. Perhaps there was a muted sense of sadness underlying this year's celebration, but that was understandable. Nita Obrenovic, Podujevo's loved and respected organizer, was no longer living. The previous winter had claimed her at the age of ninety-four, leaving the city bereft of her fierce opinions and her fiercer proportions. For sixty years Nita had worked with the citizens of Podujevo, always planning for the next contest and improving on the designs, her energies spent on making the next creation more ambitious and more life-like than the last.

Now she was dead, and sorely missed. There was no disorganization in the streets without her, the people were far too disciplined for that, but they were already falling behind schedule, and it was almost seven-twenty-five. Nita's daughter had taken over in her mother's stead, but she lacked Nita's power to galvanize the people into action. She was, in a word, too gentle for the job at hand. It required a leader who was part prophet and part ringmaster, to coax and bully and inspire the citizens into their places. Maybe, after two or three decades, and with a few more contests under her belt, Nita Obrenovic's daughter would make the grade. But for today Podujevo was behindhand; safety-checks were being overlooked; nervous looks replaced the confidence of earlier years.

Nevertheless, at six minutes before eight the first limb of Podujevo made its way out of the city to the assembly point, to wait for its fellow.

By that time the flanks were already lashed together in Popolac, and armed contingents were awaiting orders in the Town Square.

⁘

MICK WOKE PROMPTLY AT SEVEN, THOUGH there was no alarm clock in their simply furnished room at the Hotel Beograd. He lay in his bed and listened to Judd's regular breathing from the twin bed across the room. A dull morning light whimpered through the thin curtains, not encouraging an early departure. After a few minutes' staring at the cracked paintwork on the ceiling, and a while longer at the crudely carved crucifix on the opposite wall, Mick got up and went to the window. It was a dull day, as he had guessed. The sky was overcast, and the roofs of Novi Pazar were grey and featureless in the flat morning light. But beyond the roofs, to the east, he could see the hills. There was sun there. He could see shafts of light catching the blue-green of the forest, inviting a visit to their slopes.

Today maybe they would go south to Kosovska Mitrovica. There was a market there, wasn't there, and a museum? And they could drive down the valley of the

Ibar, following the road beside the river, where the hills rose wild and shining on either side. The hills, yes; today he decided they would see the hills.

It was eight-fifteen.

❖

BY NINE THE MAIN BODIES OF POPOLAC AND Podujevo were substantially assembled. In their allotted districts the limbs of both cities were ready and waiting to join their expectant torsos.

Vaslav Jelovsek capped his gloved hands over his eyes and surveyed the sky. The cloud-base had risen in the last hour, no doubt of it, and there were breaks in the clouds to the west; even, on occasion, a few glimpses of the sun. It wouldn't be a perfect day for the contest perhaps, but certainly adequate.

❖

MICK AND JUDD BREAKFASTED LATE ON hemendeks—roughly translated as ham and eggs—and several cups of good black coffee. It was brightening up, even in Novi Pazar, and their ambitions were set high. Kosovska Mitrovica by lunchtime, and maybe a visit to the hill-castle of Zvecan in the afternoon.

About nine-thirty they motored out of Novi Pazar

and took the Srbovac road south to the Ibar valley. Not a good road, but the bumps and potholes couldn't spoil the new day.

The road was empty, except for the occasional pedestrian; and in place of the maize and corn fields they'd passed on the previous day the road was flanked by undulating hills, whose sides were thickly and darkly forested. Apart from a few birds, they saw no wildlife. Even their infrequent traveling companions petered out altogether after a few miles, and the occasional farmhouse they drove by appeared locked and shuttered up. Black pigs ran unattended in the yard, with no child to feed them. Washing snapped and billowed on a sagging line, with no washerwoman in sight.

At first this solitary journey through the hills was refreshing in its lack of human contact, but as the morning drew on, an uneasiness grew on them.

"Shouldn't we have seen a signpost to Mitrovica, Mick?"

He peered at the map.

"Maybe . . ."

"—we've taken the wrong road."

"If there'd been a sign, I'd have seen it. I think we should try and get off this road, bear south a bit more—meet the valley closer to Mitrovica than we'd planned."

"How do we get off this bloody road?"

"There've been a couple of turnings . . ."

"Dirt-tracks."

"Well, it's either that or going on the way we are."

Judd pursed his lips.

"Cigarette?" he asked.

"Finished them miles back."

In front of them, the hills formed an impenetrable line. There was no sign of life ahead; no frail wisp of chimney smoke, no sound of voice or vehicle.

"All right," said Judd, "we take the next turning. Anything's better than this."

They drove on. The road was deteriorating rapidly, the potholes becoming craters, the hummocks feeling like bodies beneath the wheels.

Then:

"There!"

A turning: a palpable turning. Not a major road, certainly. In fact barely the dirt-track Judd had described the other roads as being, but it was an escape from the endless perspective of the road they were trapped on.

"This is becoming a bloody safari," said Judd as the VW began to bump and grind its way along the doleful little track.

"Where's your sense of adventure?"

"I forgot to pack it."

They were beginning to climb now, as the track wound its way up into the hills. The forest closed over them, blotting out the sky, so a shifting patchwork of light and shadow scooted over the bonnet as they drove.

There was birdsong suddenly, vacuous and optimistic, and a smell of new pine and undug earth. A fox crossed the track, up ahead, and watched a long moment as the car grumbled up towards it. Then, with the leisurely stride of a fearless prince, it sauntered away into the trees.

Wherever they were going, Mick thought, this was better than the road they'd left. Soon maybe they'd stop, and walk awhile, to find a promontory from which they could see the valley, even Novi Pazar, nestled behind them.

⁜

THE TWO MEN WERE STILL AN HOUR'S DRIVE from Popolac when the head of the contingent at last marched out of the Town Square and took up its position with the main body.

This last exit left the city completely deserted. Not even the sick or the old were neglected on this day; no one was to be denied the spectacle and the triumph of the contest. Every single citizen, however young or infirm, the blind, the crippled, babes in arms, pregnant women—all made their way up from their proud city to the stamping-ground. It was the law that they should attend: but it needed no enforcing. No citizen of either city would have missed the chance to see that sight—to experience the thrill of that contest.

The confrontation had to be total, city against city. This was the way it had always been.

So the cities went up into the hills. By noon they were gathered, the citizens of Popolac and Podujevo, in the secret well of the hills, hidden from civilized eyes, to do ancient and ceremonial battle.

Tens of thousands of hearts beat faster. Tens of thousands of bodies stretched and strained and sweated as the twin cities took their positions. The shadows of the bodies darkened tracts of land the size of small towns; the weight of their feet trampled the grass to a green milk; their movement killed animals, crushed bushes and threw down trees. The earth literally reverberated with their passage, the hills echoing with the booming din of their steps.

In the towering body of Podujevo, a few technical hitches were becoming apparent. A slight flaw in the knitting of the left flank had resulted in a weakness there: and there were consequent problems in the swivelling mechanism of the hips. It was stiffer than it should be, and the movements were not smooth. As a result there was considerable strain being put upon that region of the city. It was being dealt with bravely; after all, the contest was intended to press the contestants to their limits. But breaking point was closer than anyone would have dared to admit. The citizens were not as resilient as they had been in previous contests. A bad decade for crops had produced bodies less well-nourished, spines less supple, wills less resolute. The badly knitted flank might not

have caused an accident in itself, but further weakened by
the frailty of the competitors it set a scene for death on
an unprecedented scale.

⊰⊱

THEY STOPPED THE CAR.

"Hear that?"

Mick shook his head. His hearing hadn't been good
since he was an adolescent. Too many rock shows had
blown his eardrums to hell.

Judd got out of the car.

The birds were quieter now. The noise he'd heard as
they drove came again. It wasn't simply a noise: it was
almost a motion in the earth, a roar that seemed seated
in the substance of the hills.

Thunder, was it?

No, too rhythmical. It came again, through the soles
of the feet—

Boom.

Mick heard it this time. He leaned out of the car
window.

"It's up ahead somewhere. I hear it now."

Judd nodded.

Boom.

The earth-thunder sounded again.

"What the hell is it?" said Mick.

"Whatever it is, I want to see it—"

Judd got back into the Volkswagen, smiling.

"Sounds almost like guns," he said, starting the car. "Big guns."

⁂

THROUGH HIS RUSSIAN-MADE BINOCULARS Vaslav Jelovsek watched the starting-official raise his pistol. He saw the feather of white smoke rise from the barrel, and a second later heard the sound of the shot across the valley.

The contest had begun.

He looked up at the twin towers of Popolac and Podujevo. Heads in the clouds—well almost. They practically stretched to touch the sky. It was an awesome sight, a breath-stopping, sleep-stabbing sight. Two cities swaying and writhing and preparing to take their first steps towards each other in this ritual battle.

Of the two, Podujevo seemed the less stable. There was a slight hesitation as the city raised its left leg to begin its march. Nothing serious, just a little difficulty in coordinating hip and thigh muscles. A couple of steps and the city would find its rhythm; a couple more and its inhabitants would be moving as one creature, one perfect giant set to match its grace and power against its mirror-image.

The gunshot had sent flurries of birds up from the trees that banked the hidden valley. They rose up in celebration of the great contest, chattering their excitement as they swooped over the stamping-ground.

⁜

"DID YOU HEAR A SHOT?" ASKED JUDD.

Mick nodded.

"Military exercises . . . ?" Judd's smile had broadened. He could see the headlines already—exclusive reports of secret maneuvers in the depths of the Yugoslavian countryside. Russian tanks perhaps, tactical exercises being held out of the West's prying sight. With luck, he would be the carrier of this news.

Boom.

Boom.

There were birds in the air. The thunder was louder now.

It did sound like guns.

"It's over the next ridge . . ." said Judd.

"I don't think we should go any further."

"I have to see."

"I don't. We're not supposed to be here."

"I don't see any signs."

"They'll cart us away; deport us—I don't know—I just think—" Boom.

"I've got to see."

The words were scarcely out of his mouth when the screaming started.

⁜

PODUJEVO WAS SCREAMING: A DEATH-CRY. Someone buried in the weak flank had died of the strain, and had begun a chain of decay in the system. One man loosed his neighbor and that neighbor loosed his, spreading a cancer of chaos through the body of the city. The coherence of the towering structure deteriorated with terrifying rapidity as the failure of one part of the anatomy put unendurable pressure on the other.

The masterpiece that the good citizens of Podujevo had constructed of their own flesh and blood tottered and then—a dynamited skyscraper, it began to fall.

The broken flank spewed citizens like a slashed artery spitting blood. Then, with a graceful sloth that made the agonies of the citizens all the more horrible, it bowed towards the earth, all its limbs disassembling as it fell.

The huge head, that had brushed the clouds so recently, was flung back on its thick neck. Ten thousand mouths spoke a single scream for its vast mouth, a wordless, infinitely pitiable appeal to the sky. A howl of loss, a howl of anticipation, a howl of puzzlement. How, that scream demanded, could the day of days end like this, in a welter of falling bodies?

260

❖

"DID YOU HEAR THAT?"

It was unmistakably human, though almost deafeningly loud. Judd's stomach convulsed. He looked across at Mick, who was as white as a sheet.

Judd stopped the car.

"No," said Mick.

"Listen—for Christ's sake—"

The din of dying moans, appeals and imprecations flooded the air. It was very close.

"We've got to go on now," Mick implored.

Judd shook his head. He was prepared for some military spectacle—all the Russian army massed over the next hill—but that noise in his ears was the noise of human flesh—too human for words. It reminded him of his childhood imaginings of Hell; the endless, unspeakable torments his mother had threatened him with if he failed to embrace Christ. It was a terror he'd forgotten for twenty years. But suddenly, here it was again, fresh-faced. Maybe the pit itself gaped just over the next horizon, with his mother standing at its lip, inviting him to taste its punishments.

"If you won't drive, I will."

Mick got out of the car and crossed in front of it, glancing up the track as he did so. There was a moment's hesitation, no more than a moment's, when his eyes flickered with disbelief, before he turned towards the windscreen, his face even paler than it had been previously and said: "Jesus Christ . . ." in a voice that was thick with suppressed nausea.

His lover was still sitting behind the wheel, his head in his hands, trying to blot out memories.

"Judd . . ."

Judd looked up, slowly. Mick was staring at him like a wildman, his face shining with a sudden, icy sweat. Judd looked past him. A few meters ahead the track had mysteriously darkened, as a tide edged towards the car, a thick, deep tide of blood. Judd's reason twisted and turned to make any other sense of the sight than that inevitable conclusion. But there was no saner explanation. It was blood, in unendurable abundance, blood without end—

And now, in the breeze, there was the flavor of freshly opened carcasses: the smell out of the depths of the human body, part sweet, part savory.

Mick stumbled back to the passenger's side of the VW and fumbled weakly at the handle. The door opened suddenly and he lurched inside, his eyes glazed.

"Back up," he said.

Judd reached for the ignition. The tide of blood was already sloshing against the front wheels. Ahead, the world had been painted red.

"Drive, for fuck's sake, drive!"

Judd was making no attempt to start the car.

"We must look," he said, without conviction, "we have to."

"We don't have to do anything," said Mick, "but get the hell out of here. It's not our business . . ."

"Plane-crash—"

"There's no smoke."

"Those are human voices."

Mick's instinct was to leave well enough alone. He could read about the tragedy in a newspaper—he could see the pictures tomorrow when they were grey and grainy. Today it was too fresh, too unpredictable—

Anything could be at the end of that track, bleeding—

"We must—"

Judd started the car, while beside him Mick began to moan quietly. The VW began to edge forward, nosing through the river of blood, its wheels spinning in the queasy, foaming tide.

"No," said Mick, very quietly. "Please, no . . ."

"We must," was Judd's reply. "We must. We must."

⁎

ONLY A FEW YARDS AWAY THE SURVIVING CITY OF Popolac was recovering from its first convulsions. It stared, with a thousand eyes, at the ruins of its ritual enemy, now spread in a tangle of rope and bodies over the impacted ground, shattered forever. Popolac staggered back from the sight, its vast legs flattening the forest that bounded the stamping-ground, its arms flailing the air. But it kept its balance, even as a common insanity, woken by the horror at its feet, surged through its sinews and curdled its brain. The order went out: the body thrashed and twisted and turned from the grisly carpet of Podujevo, and fled into the hills.

As it headed into oblivion, its towering form passed between the car and the sun, throwing its cold shadow over the bloody road. Mick saw nothing through his tears, and Judd, his eyes narrowed against the sight he feared seeing around the next bend, only dimly registered that something had blotted the light for a minute. A cloud, perhaps. A flock of birds.

Had he looked up at that moment, just stolen a glance out towards the north-east, he would have seen Popolac's head, the vast, swarming head of a maddened city, disappearing below his line of vision, as it marched into the hills. He would have known that this territory was beyond his comprehension; and that there was no healing to be done in this corner of Hell. But he didn't see the city, and he and Mick's last turning-point had passed. From now on, like Popolac and its dead twin, they were lost to sanity, and to all hope of life.

⁜

THEY ROUNDED THE BEND, AND THE RUINS OF Podujevo came into sight.

Their domesticated imaginations had never conceived of a sight so unspeakably brutal.

Perhaps in the battlefields of Europe as many corpses had been heaped together: but had so many of them been women and children, locked together with the corpses of men? There had been piles of dead as high, but ever so many so recently abundant with life? There had been cities laid waste as quickly, but ever an entire city lost to the simple dictate of gravity?

It was a sight beyond sickness. In the face of it the mind slowed to a snail's pace, the forces of reason picked over the evidence with meticulous hands, searching for a flaw in it, a place where it could say:

This is not happening. This is a dream of death, not death itself.

But reason could find no weakness in the wall. This was true. It was death indeed.

Podujevo had fallen.

Thirty-eight thousand, seven hundred and sixty-five citizens were spread on the ground, or rather flung in ungainly, seeping piles. Those who had not died of the fall, or of suffocation, were dying. There would be no survivors from that city except that bundle of onlookers that had traipsed out of their homes to watch the contest. Those few Podujevians, the crippled, the sick, the ancient few, were now staring, like Mick and Judd, at the carnage, trying not to believe.

Judd was first out of the car. The ground beneath his suedes was sticky with coagulating gore. He surveyed the carnage. There was no wreckage: no sign of a plane crash, no fire, no smell of fuel. Just tens of thousands of fresh bodies, all either naked or dressed in an identical grey serge, men, women and children alike. Some of them, he could see, wore leather harnesses, tightly buckled around their upper chests, and snaking out from these contraptions were lengths of rope, miles and miles of it. The closer he looked, the more he saw of the extraordinary system of knots and lashings that still held the bodies together. For some reason these people had been tied together, side by side. Some were yoked on their neighbors' shoulders, straddling them like boys playing at horseback riding. Others were locked arm in arm, knitted together with threads of rope in a wall of muscle and bone. Yet others were trussed in a ball, with their heads tucked between their knees. All were in some way connected up with their fellows, tied together as though in some insane collective bondage game.

Another shot.

Mick looked up.

Across the field a solitary man, dressed in a drab overcoat, was walking amongst the bodies with a revolver, dispatching the dying. It was a pitifully inadequate act of mercy, but he went on nevertheless, choosing the suffering children first. Emptying the revolver, filling it again, emptying it, filling it, emptying it—

Mick let go.

He yelled at the top of his voice over the moans of the injured.

"What is this?"

The man looked up from his appalling duty, his face as dead-grey as his coat.

"Uh?" he grunted, frowning at the two interlopers through his thick spectacles.

"What's happened here?" Mick shouted across at him. It felt good to shout, it felt good to sound angry at the man. Maybe he was to blame. It would be a fine thing, just to have someone to blame.

"Tell us—" Mick said. He could hear the tears throbbing in his voice. "Tell us, for God's sake. Explain."

Grey-coat shook his head. He didn't understand a word this young idiot was saying. It was English he spoke, and that's all he knew. Mick began to walk towards him, feeling all the time the eyes of the dead on him. Eyes like black, shining gems set in broken faces: eyes looking at him upside down, on heads severed from their seating. Eyes in heads that had solid howls for voices. Eyes in heads beyond howls, beyond breath.

Thousands of eyes.

He reached Grey-coat, whose gun was almost empty. He had taken off his spectacles and thrown them aside. He too was weeping, little jerks ran through his big, ungainly body.

At Mick's feet, somebody was reaching for him. He didn't want to look, but the hand touched his shoe and he had no choice but to see its owner. A young man, lying like a flesh swastika, every joint smashed. A child lay under him, her bloody legs poking out like two pink sticks.

He wanted the man's revolver, to stop the hand from touching him. Better still he wanted a machine-gun, a flame-thrower, anything to wipe the agony away.

As he looked up from the broken body, Mick saw Grey-coat raise the revolver.

"Judd—" he said, but as the word left his lips the muzzle of the revolver was slipped into Grey-coat's mouth and the trigger was pulled.

Grey-coat had saved the last bullet for himself. The back of his head opened like a dropped egg, the shell of his skull flying off. His body went limp and sank to the ground, the revolver still between his lips.

"We must—" began Mick, saying the words to nobody. "We must . . ."

What was the imperative? In this situation, what *must* they do?

"We must—"

Judd was behind him.

"Help—" he said to Mick.

"Yes. We must get help. We must—"

"Go."

Go! That was what they must do. On any pretext, for any fragile, cowardly reason, they must go. Get out of the battlefield, get out of the reach of a dying hand with a wound in place of a body.

"We have to tell the authorities. Find a town. Get help—"

"Priests," said Mick. "They need priests."

It was absurd, to think of giving the Last Rites to so many people. It would take an army of priests, a water cannon filled with holy water, a loudspeaker to pronounce the benedictions.

They turned away, together, from the horror, and wrapped their arms around each other, then picked their way through the carnage to the car.

It was occupied.

Vaslav Jelovsek was sitting behind the wheel, and trying to start the Volkswagen. He turned the ignition key once. Twice. Third time the engine caught and the wheels spun in the crimson mud as he put her into reverse and backed down the track. Vaslav saw the Englishmen running towards the car, cursing him. There was no help for it—he didn't want to steal the vehicle, but he had work to do. He had been a referee, he had been responsible for the contest, and the safety of the contestants. One of the heroic cities had already fallen. He must do everything in his power to prevent Popolac from following its twin. He must chase Popolac, and reason with it. Talk it down out of its terrors with quiet words and promises. If he failed there would be another disaster the equal of the one in front of him, and his conscience was already broken enough.

Mick was still chasing the VW, shouting at Jelovsek. The thief took no notice, concentrating on maneuvering the car back down the narrow, slippery track. Mick was losing the chase rapidly. The car had begun to pick up speed. Furious, but without the breath to speak his fury, Mick stood in the road, hands on his knees, heaving and sobbing.

"Bastard!" said Judd.

Mick looked down the track. Their car had already disappeared.

"Fucker couldn't even drive properly."

"We have . . . we have . . . to catch . . . up . . ." said Mick through gulps of breath.

"How?"

"On foot . . ."

"We haven't even got a map . . . it's in the car."

"Jesus . . . Christ . . . Almighty."

They walked down the track together, away from the field.

After a few meters the tide of blood began to peter out. Just a few congealing rivulets dribbled on towards the main road. Mick and Judd followed the bloody tire marks to the junction.

The Srbovac road was empty in both directions. The tire marks showed a left turn. "He's gone deeper into the hills," said Judd, staring along the lovely road towards the blue-green distance. "He's out of his mind!"

"Do we go back the way we came?"

"It'll take us all night on foot."

"We'll hop a lift."

Judd shook his head: his face was slack and his look lost. "Don't you see, Mick? They all knew this was happening. The people in the farms—they got the hell out while those people went crazy up there. There'll be no cars along this road, I'll lay you anything—except maybe a couple of shit-dumb tourists like us—and no tourist would stop for the likes of us."

He was right. They looked like butchers—splattered with blood. Their faces were shining with grease, their eyes maddened.

"We'll have to walk," said Judd, "the way he went."

He pointed along the road. The hills were darker now; the sun had suddenly gone out on their slopes.

Mick shrugged. Either way he could see they had a night on the road ahead of them. But he wanted to walk somewhere—anywhere, as long as he put distance between him and the dead.

⁕

IN POPOLAC A KIND OF PEACE REIGNED. INSTEAD of a frenzy of panic, there was a numbness, a sheep-like acceptance of the world as it was. Locked in their positions, strapped, roped and harnessed to each other in a living system that allowed for no single voice to be louder than any other, nor any back to labor less than its neighbor, they let an insane consensus replace the tranquil voice of reason. They were convulsed into one mind, one thought, one ambition. They became, in the space of a few moments, the single-minded giant whose image they had so brilliantly re-created. The illusion of petty individuality was swept away in an irresistible tide of collective feeling—not a mob's passion, but a telepathic surge that dissolved the voices of thousands into one irresistible command.

And the voice said: Go!

The voice said: take this horrible sight away, where I need never see it again.

Popolac turned away into the hills, its legs taking strides half a mile long. Each man, woman and child in that seething tower was sightless. They saw only through the eyes of the city. They were thoughtless, but to think the city's thoughts. And they believed themselves deathless, in their lumbering, relentless strength. Vast and mad and deathless.

⚜

TWO MILES ALONG THE ROAD MICK AND JUDD smelt petrol in the air, and a little further along they came upon the VW. It had overturned in the reed-

272

clogged drainage ditch at the side of the road. It had not caught fire.

The driver's door was open, and the body of Vaslav Jelovsek had tumbled out. His face was calm in unconsciousness. There seemed to be no sign of injury, except for a small cut or two on his sober face. They gently pulled the thief out of the wreckage and up out of the filth of the ditch onto the road. He moaned a little as they fussed about him, rolling Mick's sweater up to pillow his head and removing the man's jacket and tie.

Quite suddenly, he opened his eyes.

He stared at them both.

"Are you all right?" Mick asked.

The man said nothing for a moment. He seemed not to understand.

Then:

"English?" he said. His accent was thick, but the question was quite clear.

"Yes."

"I heard your voices. English."

He frowned and winced.

"Are you in pain?" said Judd.

The man seemed to find this amusing.

"Am I in pain?" he repeated, his face screwed up in a mixture of agony and delight.

"I shall die," he said, through gritted teeth.

"No," said Mick. "You're all right—"

The man shook his head, his authority absolute.

"I shall die," he said again, the voice full of determination. "I want to die."

Judd crouched closer to him. His voice was weaker by the moment.

"Tell us what to do," he said. The man had closed his eyes. Judd shook him awake, roughly.

"Tell us," he said again, his show of compassion rapidly disappearing. "Tell us what this is all about."

"About?" said the man, his eyes still closed. "It was a fall, that's all. Just a fall . . ."

"What fell?"

"The city. Podujevo. My city."

"What did it fall from?"

"Itself, of course."

The man was explaining nothing; just answering one riddle with another.

"Where were you going?" Mick inquired, trying to sound as unaggressive as possible.

"After Popolac," said the man.

"Popolac?" said Judd.

Mick began to see some sense in the story.

"Popolac is another city. Like Podujevo. Twin cities. They're on the map—"

"Where's the city now?" said Judd.

Vaslav Jelovsek seemed to choose to tell the truth. There was a moment when he hovered between dying with a riddle on his lips, and living long enough to

274

unburden his story. What did it matter if the tale was told now? There could never be another contest: all that was over.

"They came to fight," he said, his voice now very soft, "Popolac and Podujevo. They come every ten years—"

"Fight?" said Judd. "You mean all those people were slaughtered?"

Vaslav shook his head.

"No, no. They fell. I told you."

"Well, how do they fight?" Mick said.

"Go into the hills," was the only reply.

Vaslav opened his eyes a little. The faces that loomed over him were exhausted and sick. They had suffered, these innocents. They deserved some explanation.

"As giants," he said. "They fought as giants. They made a body out of their bodies, do you understand? The frame, the muscles, the bone, the eyes, nose, teeth all made of men and women."

"He's delirious," said Judd.

"You go into the hills," the man repeated. "See for yourselves how true it is."

"Even supposing—" Mick began.

Vaslav interrupted him, eager to be finished. "They were good at the game of giants. It took many centuries of practice: every ten years making the figure larger and larger. One always ambitious to be larger than the other. Ropes to tie them all together, flawlessly. Sinews . . . ligaments . . . There was food in its belly . . . there were pipes from the loins, to take away the waste. The best-sighted sat in the eye-sockets, the best voiced in the mouth and throat. You wouldn't believe the engineering of it."

"I don't," said Judd, and stood up.

"It is the body of the state," said Vaslav, so softly his voice was barely above a whisper, "it is the shape of our lives."

There was a silence. Small clouds passed over the road, soundlessly shedding their mass to the air.

"It was a miracle," he said. It was as if he realized the true enormity of the fact for the first time. "It was a miracle."

It was enough. Yes. It was quite enough.

His mouth closed, the words said, and he died.

Mick felt this death more acutely than the thousands they had fled from; or rather this death was the key to unlock the anguish he felt for them all.

Whether the man had chosen to tell a fantastic lie as he died, or whether this story was in some way true, Mick felt useless in the face of it. His imagination was too narrow to encompass the idea. His brain ached with the thought of it, and his compassion cracked under the weight of misery he felt.

They stood on the road, while the clouds scudded by, their vague, grey shadows passing over them towards the enigmatic hills.

⁂

It was twilight.

Popolac could stride no further. It felt exhaustion in every muscle. Here and there in its huge anatomy deaths had occurred; but there was no grieving in the city for its deceased cells. If the dead were in the interior, the corpses were allowed to hang from their harnesses. If they formed the skin of the city they were unbuckled from their positions and released, to plunge into the forest below.

The giant was not capable of pity. It had no ambition but to continue until it ceased.

As the sun slunk out of sight Popolac rested, sitting on a small hillock, nursing its huge head in its huge hands.

The stars were coming out, with their familiar caution. Night was approaching, mercifully bandaging up the wounds of the day, blinding eyes that had seen too much.

Popolac rose to its feet again, and began to move, step by booming step. It would not be long, surely, before fatigue overcame it: before it could lie down in the tomb of some lost valley and die.

But for a space yet it must walk on, each step more agonizingly slow than the last, while the night bloomed black around its head.

✢

MICK WANTED TO BURY THE CAR THIEF, somewhere on the edge of the forest. Judd, however, pointed out that burying a body might seem, in tomorrow's saner light, a little suspicious. And besides, wasn't it absurd to concern themselves with one corpse when there were literally thousands of them lying a few miles from where they stood?

The body was left to lie, therefore, and the car to sink deeper into the ditch.

They began to walk again.

It was cold, and colder by the moment, and they were hungry. But the few houses they passed were all deserted, locked and shuttered, every one.

"What did he mean?" said Mick, as they stood looking at another locked door.

"He was talking metaphor—"

"All that stuff about giants?"

"It was some Trotskyist tripe—" Judd insisted.

"I don't think so."

"I know so. It was his deathbed speech, he'd probably been preparing for years."

"I don't think so," Mick said again, and began walking back towards the road.

"Oh, how's that?" Judd was at his back.

"He wasn't toeing some party line."

"Are you saying you think there's some giant around here someplace? For God's sake!"

Mick turned to Judd. His face was difficult to see in the twilight. But his voice was sober with belief.

"Yes. I think he was telling the truth."

"That's absurd. That's ridiculous. No."

Judd hated Mick that moment. Hated his naïveté, his passion to believe any half-witted story if it had a whiff of romance about it. And this? This was the worst, the most preposterous . . .

"No," he said again. "No. No. No."

The sky was porcelain smooth, and the outline of the hills black as pitch. "I'm fucking freezing," said Mick out of the ink. "Are you staying here or walking with me?"

Judd shouted: "We're not going to find anything this way."

"Well, it's a long way back."

"We're just going deeper into the hills."

"Do what you like—I'm walking."

His footsteps receded: the dark encased him.

After a minute, Judd followed.

❖

THE NIGHT WAS CLOUDLESS AND BITTER. THEY walked on, their collars up against the chill, their feet swollen in their shoes. Above them the whole sky had become a parade of stars. A triumph of spilled light, from which the eye could make as many patterns as it had patience for. After a while, they slung their tired arms around each other, for comfort and warmth.

About eleven o'clock, they saw the glow of a window in the distance.

The woman at the door of the stone cottage didn't smile, but she understood their condition, and let them in. There seemed to be no purpose in trying to explain to either the woman or her crippled husband what they had seen. The cottage had no telephone, and there was no sign of a vehicle, so even had they found some way to express themselves, nothing could be done.

With mimes and face-pullings they explained that they were hungry and exhausted. They tried further to explain that they were lost, cursing themselves for leaving their phrase book in the VW. She didn't seem to understand very much of what they said, but sat them down beside a blazing fire and put a pan of food on the stove to heat.

They ate thick unsalted pea soup and eggs, and occasionally smiled their thanks at the woman. Her husband sat beside the fire, making no attempt to talk, or even look at the visitors.

The food was good. It buoyed their spirits.

They would sleep until morning and then begin the long trek back. By dawn the bodies in the field would be being quantified, identified, parceled up and dispatched to their families. The air would be full of reassuring noises, canceling out the moans that still rang in their ears. There would be helicopters, lorry loads of men organizing the clearing-up operations. All the rites and paraphernalia of a civilized disaster.

And in a while, it would be palatable. It would become part of their history: a tragedy, of course, but one they could explain, classify and learn to live with. All would be well, yes, all would be well. Come morning.

The sleep of sheer fatigue came on them suddenly. They lay where they had fallen, still sitting at the table, their heads on their crossed arms. A litter of empty bowls and bread crusts surrounded them.

They knew nothing. Dreamt nothing. Felt nothing.

Then the thunder began.

In the earth, in the deep earth, a rhythmical tread, as of a titan, that came, by degrees, closer and closer.

The woman woke her husband. She blew out the lamp and went to the door. The night sky was luminous with stars: the hills black on every side.

The thunder still sounded: a full half minute between every boom, but louder now. And louder with every new step.

They stood at the door together, husband and wife, and listened to the night-hills echo back and forth with the sound. There was no lightning to accompany the thunder.

Just the boom—

Boom—

Boom—

It made the ground shake: it threw dust down from the door-lintel, and rattled the window-latches.

Boom—

Boom—

They didn't know what approached, but whatever shape it took, and whatever it intended, there seemed no sense in running from it. Where they stood, in the pitiful shelter of their cottage, was as safe as any nook of the forest. How could they choose, out of a hundred thousand trees, which would be standing when the thunder had passed? Better to wait: and watch.

The wife's eyes were not good, and she doubted what she saw when the blackness of the hill changed shape and reared up to block the stars. But her husband had seen it too: the unimaginably huge head, vaster in the deceiving darkness, looming up and up, dwarfing the hills themselves with ambition.

He fell to his knees, babbling a prayer, his arthritic legs twisted beneath him.

His wife screamed: no words she knew could keep this monster at bay—no prayer, no plea, had power over it.

In the cottage, Mick woke and his outstretched arm, twitching with a sudden cramp, wiped the plate and the lamp off the table.

They smashed.

Judd woke.

The screaming outside had stopped. The woman had

disappeared from the doorway into the forest. Any tree, any tree at all, was better than this sight. Her husband still let a string of prayers dribble from his slack mouth, as the great leg of the giant rose to take another step—

Boom—

The cottage shook. Plates danced and smashed off the dresser. A clay pipe rolled from the mantelpiece and shattered in the ashes of the hearth.

The lovers knew the noise that sounded in their substance: that earth-thunder.

Mick reached for Judd, and took him by the shoulder.

"You see," he said, his teeth blue-grey in the darkness of the cottage. "See? See?"

There was a kind of hysteria bubbling behind his words. He ran to the door, stumbling over a chair in the dark. Cursing and bruised he staggered out into the night—

Boom—

The thunder was deafening. This time it broke all the windows in the cottage. In the bedroom one of the roof-joists cracked and flung debris downstairs.

Judd joined his lover at the door. The old man was now face down on the ground, his sick and swollen fingers curled, his begging lips pressed to the damp soil.

Mick was looking up, towards the sky. Judd followed his gaze.

There was a place that showed no stars. It was a darkness in the shape of a man, a vast, broad human frame, a colossus that soared up to meet heaven. It was not quite a perfect giant. Its outline was not tidy; it seethed and swarmed.

He seemed broader too, this giant, than any real man. His legs were abnormally thick and stumpy, and his arms were not long. The hands, as they clenched and unclenched, seemed oddly jointed and over-delicate for its torso.

Then it raised one huge, flat foot and placed it on the earth, taking a stride towards them.

Boom—

The step brought the roof collapsing in on the cottage. Everything that the car thief had said was true. Popolac was a city and a giant; and it had gone into the hills . . .

Now their eyes were becoming accustomed to the night light. They could see in ever more horrible detail the way this monster was constructed. It was a masterpiece of human engineering: a man made entirely of men. Or rather, a sexless giant, made of men and women and children. All the citizens of Popolac writhed and strained in the body of this flesh-knitted giant, their muscles stretched to breaking point, their bones close to snapping.

They could see how the architects of Popolac had subtly altered the proportions of the human body; how the thing had been made squatter to lower its center of gravity; how its legs had been made elephantine to bear the weight of the torso; how the head was sunk low onto the wide shoulders, so that the problems of a weak neck had been minimized.

Despite these malformations, it was horribly life-like. The bodies that were bound together to make its surface were naked but for their harnesses, so that its surface glistened in the starlight, like one vast human torso. Even the muscles were well copied, though simplified. They could see the way the roped bodies pushed and pulled against each other in solid cords of flesh and bone. They could see the intertwined people that made up the body: the backs like turtles packed together to offer the sweep of the pectorals; the lashed and knotted acrobats at the joints of the arms and the legs alike; rolling and unwinding to articulate the city.

But surely the most amazing sight of all was the face.

Cheeks of bodies; cavernous eye-sockets in which heads stared, five bound together for each eyeball; a broad, flat nose and a mouth that opened and closed, as the muscles of the jaw bunched and hollowed rhythmically. And from that mouth, lined with teeth of bald children, the voice of the giant, now only a weak copy of its former powers, spoke a single note of idiot music.

Popolac walked and Popolac sang.

Was there ever a sight in Europe the equal of it?

They watched, Mick and Judd, as it took another step towards them.

The old man had wet his pants. Blubbering and

begging, he dragged himself away from the ruined cottage into the surrounding trees, dragging his dead legs after him.

The Englishmen remained where they stood, watching the spectacle as it approached. Neither dread nor horror touched them now, just an awe that rooted them to the spot. They knew this was a sight they could never hope to see again; this was the apex—after this there was only common experience. Better to stay then, though every step brought death nearer, better to stay and see the sight while it was still there to be seen. And if it killed them, this monster, then at least they would have glimpsed a miracle, known this terrible majesty for a brief moment. It seemed a fair exchange.

Popolac was within two steps of the cottage. They could see the complexities of its structure quite clearly. The faces of the citizens were becoming detailed: white, sweat-wet and content in their weariness. Some hung dead from their harnesses, their legs swinging back and forth like the hanged. Others, children particularly, had ceased to obey their training, and had relaxed their positions, so that the form of the body was degenerating, beginning to seethe with the boils of rebellious cells.

Yet it still walked, each step an incalculable effort of coordination and strength.

Boom—

The step that trod the cottage came sooner than they thought.

Mick saw the leg raised; saw the faces of the people in the shin and ankle and foot—they were as big as he was now—all huge men chosen to take the full weight of this great creation. Many were dead. The bottom of the foot, he could see, was a jigsaw of crushed and bloody bodies, pressed to death under the weight of their fellow citizens.

The foot descended with a roar.

In a matter of seconds the cottage was reduced to splinters and dust.

Popolac blotted the sky utterly. It was, for a moment, the whole world, heaven and earth, its presence filled the senses to overflowing. At this proximity one look could not encompass it, the eye had to range backwards and forwards over its mass to take it all in, and even then the mind refused to accept the whole truth.

A whirling fragment of stone, flung off from the cottage as it collapsed, struck Judd full in the face. In his head he heard the killing stroke like a ball hitting a wall: a play-yard death. No pain: no remorse. Out like a light, a tiny, insignificant light; his death-cry lost in the pandemonium, his body hidden in the smoke and darkness. Mick neither saw nor heard Judd die.

He was too busy staring at the foot as it settled for a moment in the ruins of the cottage, while the other leg mustered the will to move.

Mick took his chance. Howling like a banshee, he ran towards the leg, longing to embrace the monster. He stumbled in the wreckage, and stood again, bloodied, to reach for the foot before it was lifted and he was left behind. There was a clamor of agonized breath as the message came to the foot that it must move; Mick saw the muscles of the shin bunch and marry as the leg began to lift. He made one last lunge at the limb as it began to leave the ground, snatching a harness or a rope, or human hair, or flesh itself—anything to catch this passing miracle and be part of it. Better to go with it wherever it was going, serve it in its purpose, whatever that might be; better to die with it than live without it.

He caught the foot, and found a safe purchase on its ankle. Screaming his sheer ecstasy at his success he felt the great leg raised, and glanced down through the swirling dust to the spot where he had stood, already receding as the limb climbed.

The earth was gone from beneath him. He was a hitchhiker with a god: the mere life he had left was nothing to him now, or ever. He would live with this thing, yes, he would live with it—seeing it and seeing it and eating it with his eyes until he died of sheer gluttony.

He screamed and howled and swung on the ropes, drinking up his triumph. Below, far below, he glimpsed Judd's body, curled up pale on the dark ground, irretrievable. Love and life and sanity were gone, gone like the memory of his name, or his sex, or his ambition.

It all meant nothing. Nothing at all.

Boom—

Boom—

Popolac walked, the noise of its steps receding to the east. Popolac walked, the hum of its voice lost in the night.

❖

AFTER A DAY, BIRDS CAME, FOXES CAME, FLIES, butterflies, wasps came. Judd moved, Judd shifted, Judd gave birth. In his belly maggots warmed themselves, in a vixen's den the good flesh of his thigh was fought over. After that, it was quick. The bones yellowing, the bones crumbling: soon, an empty space which he had once filled with breath and opinions.

Darkness, light, darkness, light. He interrupted neither with his name.

Ready to find
your next great read?

Let us help.

Visit prh.com/nextread

Penguin
Random
House